SNOW FLAKE

A NOVEL

R. T. WILEY

To Tom
Best wishes
R. T. Wiley
4-14-17

SNOW FLAKE, a novel

This is a work of fiction. Names, characters, businesses, places, events, and incidents are either products of the author's imagination or used in a fictitious manner. Any resemblance or similarity to persons living or dead or actual events is purely coincidental.

ISBN-13: 978-1516940554
ISBN-10: 1516940555

Credits: Cover design: @NewGalleryPublishing.com
Cover photo: © Lledo @ Courtesy Shutterstock.com
Editing: @NewGalleryPublishing.com
Book design: @NewGalleryPublishing.com
Author photo courtesy R. T. Wiley

Interior text is set in Palatino with headers set in COPPERPLATE GOTHIC LIGHT. Title pages are set in FELIX TITLING.

Snow Flake, a novel, is also available for immediate download as an eBook from Amazon.com (for Kindle e-readers) and from Smashwords.com for all other e-readers.

For a signed copy of this book, contact the author at azwiley@gmail.com.

SNOW ❄ FLAKE

1

Twenty-four hours ago, Prisoner Elroy J. Hastings WAS transferred from death row to the death house, which was located separate and apart from the prison. The guards were keeping a close vigil on Hastings to prevent any suicide attempts. The prison chaplain had arrived about eight hours ago to provide him comfort in any way he legally could.

Prison guards had been testing the electric chair to ensure it was working properly. The telephone in the death chamber connected to the governor's office had also been checked. Some prisoners might receive a stay of execution, but there was slim chance for Hastings.

The design of the electric chair had changed little since its development in New York in 1889. Later, in Nebraska it had dubbed "Old Sparky" by the inmates. The chair was made of wood so it would not conduct current. The electricity would flow through the prisoner's head piece, and exit out the leg connections, completing the circuit.

The electric chair was declining in favor as one of several forms of execution used in the United States. It was once the custom to offer the prisoner his favorite meal on the evening before the fatal date, but times were changing. More common now, the condemned prisoner would receive whatever was served that day for dinner at the prison mess hall. Besides, Elroy wasn't very hungry, and he wasn't going to get much sleep that night either.

A heavy metal door opened. Ten people entered the anteroom silently, walking in single file; the only sounds were a slight rustle of clothing as six men and four women took their seats in the straight-backed wooden chairs. Chairs scraped against the concrete floor; one man coughed, and another cleared his throat. In here, muted sounds of voices raised in protest outside were barely audible.

The parents of Elroy Hastings were seated in the front row beside Bernard and Sally Dunlap.

Arnold Hastings, Elroy's father, held his wife as she cried softly, her head pressed against his shoulder. "Betty, are you sure you want to be here?" he asked.

"He's our son. But he done wrong, and he must pay for that," she said.

Hastings patted her on the shoulder, trying to ease her anguish.

The room was poorly lit, and the air seemed stale. The metal door swung shut with a solid "click." From a speaker box mounted high in the corner of the room a voice announced: "We're ready." Curtains opened on the glass wall before the first row of seats, and the execution room was in full view.

Strapped in the electric chair was Elroy Hastings, a man who had been found guilty of the savage rape and murder of ten-year-old Kelly Dunlap. The electric chair looked too large for Elroy's body, but then, it had been built to accommodate people of different sizes. Three uniformed prison guards, the warden, a doctor, and a priest were in the room with him. The priest was standing to one side, praying quietly. The guards were busy, working to strap Elroy securely to the chair. There were multiple belts and buckles and a strap that secured his head. He didn't put up any resistance. He sat with his eyes closed, tears running down his face.

When the guards were finished they stepped aside.

The warden approached the prisoner. "Elroy, do you have any last words?"

Elroy looked from the warden to the one-way glass window in front of him. "Mama... Daddy.... I know I've disappointed you just about all my life, and now I will go meet my maker. Mr. and Mrs. Dunlap, I'm sorry for what I did to your daughter Kelly. When I get to heaven, I will tell her how sorry I feel." He closed his eyes again and waited.

The warden signaled to a guard in an enclosed booth at the rear of the room. With the single pull of a handle, electricity surged through Elroy's body. He jerked uncontrollably. Smoke appeared around the top of his head where they had placed a wet natural sponge under the head cap.

Mrs. Dunlap jumped to her feet screaming. "Fry, you son of a bitch! Fry for what you did to my little girl. You're not going go to meet your maker! You're going to the depths of hell! Our Kelly would never forgive you for what you took from her—and neither will we!"

Her outburst startled everyone in the viewing area, but most folks would have felt the same way, if they had been following the events leading up to this particular execution.

He did fry. To the attorney Scott St. Germain, it sounded like bacon in a frying pan.

Elroy's skin had turned the color of a person with a bad sun burn. He had vomited too; drool was running from his mouth. Exactly forty-two seconds after the execution had begun, the warden signaled for the electricity to be shut off.

The doctor had to wait until the body had cooled before entering to pronounce Elroy Hastings dead. He turned and slowly, deliberately, closed the curtains. The women in the viewing room had covered their eyes; some were weeping. The men stared about in a state of shock and disbelief.

~

I filed out with the rest of the people who had viewed the execution, out to the waiting reporters and to those outside protesting against the death penalty. The reporters were asking all sorts of stupid questions, as they usually do, and sticking their microphones into our faces. They were such a bunch of jerks.

This was the first time I had attended one of these and I hoped it would be the last. I'm not normally a squeamish kind of guy, but this ordeal left my stomach in knots.

Elroy's parents climbed into their car and drove away. The Dunlap family tried their best to avoid the pursuing reporters. Finally the police stepped in and stopped the insensitive media, who insisted on asking those all important questions. "How do you feel?" they kept on asking. And, "Does this bring you any closure?"

People like that were assholes. They had absolutely no sensitivity and should not have been allowed near the grieving parents, either the Dunlaps or the Hastings.

I had been invited to the execution by the prison warden and the governor of the other state. It was customary to invite several civilian witnesses to attend any execution, but the rage and indignation surrounding a child's rape and murder always created special morbid interest. It had been a long drive because of the change of venue. It would feel mighty good to get back to my home in Wisconsin.

My name is Scott St. Germain. I'm an attorney in the small city of Marinette, Wisconsin, that has a population of around 15,000. The interstate bridge spans the Menominee River that separates Marinette, Wisconsin, from Menominee, Michigan, located in the Upper Peninsula. Combined with the 10,000 residents on the Michigan side, Marinette and Menominee are locally known as the "Twin Cities." They both grace the shores of Lake Michigan by way of Green Bay—not the city, just the bay. The winters are brutal. However, the summers are wonderful if you don't mind the humidity and mosquitoes.

My law practice consists of myself, my part-time office gal Simone, and a local private investigator by the name of Donald Doyle. Our town more commonly calls him "Digger" Doyle. He picked up the nickname because of his unrelenting efforts to dig up dirt on anyone he needed to, and together we make a pretty good team. Our work often takes us out of the area. I have worked on cases in Lower Michigan and in Wisconsin, and as far south as the Illinois border.

I actually prefer to work reasonably close to home, because I'm more familiar with the people and the territory. My favorite restaurant and watering hole is The Crew's Quarters. Since it's just a few blocks away from my office I frequent it as often as I can.

My home is a grand old, turn of the century house overlooking the Menominee River. Shortly after purchasing the gracious two-story house, I converted the front half of the ground floor into my office. My living quarters are upstairs.

The original owners had been a family of means and had immigrated from the old country. They had settled here and operated a large lumber business. Their old home was beautifully constructed by craftsmen of a bygone era. The workmanship is exquisite in every way.

It was late in the afternoon when I arrived home. Pulling into the driveway, I parked in the back as usual. Out there I keep a motor home that has two slide outs; when they're extended it's quite comfortable. I use the RV for cases out of town and tow my Jeep.

Gingerly I entered the back door and walked to my office, images of the execution still flashing through my mind. Right then, I felt like Elroy's execution would be burned into my brain forever.

Simone had left me a couple of Post-it notes stuck to the phone so I wouldn't miss them. It was a system of communication that worked well for us.

The first note read: "Call Del Morgan about joining the Bayside Golf Club." The other one was from Mrs. Moorland, a widow who lived on the other side of town. Simone had neatly included a return number at the bottom. Del had been after me to join the club for months.

I wasn't really big on joining anything right now; I needed time to unwind from the long, grueling case of *Dunlap vs. Hastings.* I had represented the Dunlap family. The case had taken a lot out of me, but it was worth it. Elroy Hastings got what he had coming to him. It had been a long trial, but at least it was a swift verdict.

In the kitchen I made myself a toasted cheese sandwich and popped open a can of beer. I carried them back to the office, careful not to spill anything or I would catch hell from Simone. Sometimes I think that she thinks she's my mother rather than my part-time office girl. I dialed Mrs. Moorland's number and tucked the receiver between my ear and my shoulder, my sandwich in one hand and the beer in the other.

"Hello, Mrs. Moorland. This is Scott St. Germain. I received a message that you called earlier."

"Yes, Mr. St. Germain. I was wondering if I could hire you to find my dog. He's a small brown Chihuahua. I call him Cuddles. I'm sure he was kidnapped by one of the neighbors. I'll be willing to pay you to find him." Her voice was breaking with tears and emotion. He's been gone now for five days—my dog is like my child to me."

"Mrs. Moorland, I'm so sorry for your loss. However, to take on any kind of a case, I require a $500 retainer fee and after that $300 an hour." I paused a moment. "And, Mrs. Moorland, that does not include expenses."

"Oh, dear. That's a lot of money. I just don't know what to do," she replied and hung up abruptly.

There was deep concern in her voice, and it left me feeling like a greedy jerk trying to take advantage of a poor, old widow lady. I finished my sandwich and beer and decided to take my self-loathing out on the weeds in my yard. Attacking them, weed whacker in hand, twenty minutes later I was finished and felt somewhat better.

The next morning that damn execution was still on my mind. And it was still bothering me the way I had handled the conversation with the widow lady. I decided to drive out to her home on Carney Avenue. There were kids and dogs along the street but none of the dogs looked like a Chihuahua. I headed for the local dog pound in hopes that someone had turned him in. Inside, there was a young girl at the counter.

She spoke first. "Good morning, sir. Are you here to adopt a pet?" There was cheer and hope in her voice.

"No thanks. I'm looking for a lost one," I replied rather sharply.

"A dog or cat?"

"Dog—a Chihuahua."

"I think you're in luck. We had one come in a few days ago," she said. "I believe he's scheduled to be put down tomorrow."

"Is he brown?"

The girl smiled. "Yes, as a matter of fact he is. I'll take you out to see him after we finish the paperwork."

I filled out the papers and paid the fee, up front, no further question asked.

"Here," she said. "Just follow me out back to the kennels."

We stopped at a large pen. A small, scroungy-looking mutt that had been through rough times stared back at us. He was dirty and smelly, and mud was stuck to his fur.

"Did he have a collar or any ID when he was dropped off?" I asked. "Maybe a microchip?"

"Nope. He was pretty much as you see him. He's all yours." She opened the cage, and the dog started trembling all over. The girl placed him in my arms, and he promptly peed on my shirt. It was like holding a one-pound leaking vibrator; his shaking got even worse.

I couldn't take him back to the widow lady looking like this. "Could you recommend a good dog groomer?" I asked while the girl from the dog pound was still there.

"Certainly." She scribbled an address and a phone number on the back of my business card.

I called the groomer and asked if she had an opening for an appointment.

"Lucky you called," she said. "I just had a cancellation."

Sure, I thought with some amusement. In the town of Marinette, dog groomers probably always "just had a cancellation." I set aside my cynicism for the moment. "I'll be right there."

The dog peed again. This time it was on my car seat while we were on the way to the groomers.

The lady groomer took one look at the disheveled dog; I could tell by the expression on her face that she felt sorry for Cuddles.

"I'll have him spiffed up in no time," she said. "You can pick him up in an hour."

So far I had spent one hundred dollars on this hairball. However, I'll have to admit, I was feeling a lot better about how it would help the widow's frame of mind. An hour later, back at the groomer's place, I couldn't believe it was the same dog. He was clean, polished, and even smelled good, but he still was trembling.

I pulled up in front of Mrs. Moorland's home, parked, and snapped the leash on Cuddles' new collar, then walked him up to the front door and rang the bell.

"Hello, Mrs. Moorland. I'm Scott St. Germain. Good news! I'm returning Cuddles to you," I said triumphantly.

She glanced down at the dog. "That's not Cuddles!" she exclaimed. "I found Cuddles dead under a heavy pot. He was behind the garage in the backyard. The pot must have fallen off the shelf and killed him. I went to a pet store yesterday and bought another dog." She quickly closed the door in my face.

Damn, what the hell should I do now?

My new one-pound, guard dog is named K9, and he has a sweater thus inscribed to prove it. He depends on me for his daily sustenance and sleeps on a pillow in my office. Simone and I are working on how teaching him to do his business outside.

Simone works Monday, Wednesday, and Friday. On her days off, she's attending junior college where she's majoring in business. She and K9 have become the best of friends.

2

The phone rang three times before Simone picked up. "Scott St. Germain, Attorney at Law. May I help you?" she answered cheerily. "One moment, please." After tapping the hold button she handed me the phone.

"Boss, a Mr. Bret Singer is asking for you. He's the manager at the marina where your yacht is docked. He sounds upset."

I picked up the phone in my office. "Hey, Bret. What's going on?"

"Mr. St. Germain, it seems that someone broke in through our security gate last night and spray-painted the words 'Dead Man' on the hull of your yacht—it's in bright red letters. They must have climbed over the fence or walked in behind another boat owner last night."

"When did you discover it?"

"About thirty minutes ago. I would have called you then, but I needed to see if other boats had been damaged."

I considered my options for a moment. "Bret? Do me a favor. Could you take a picture of it? Send it to my cell phone. I'll call my insurance guy and pass it on to him." Who in the hell would do something like that? I kept wondering about it, and the thought really bugged me. The message must have been meant for me—otherwise they would have damaged other craft.

Bret's cell phone message and photo arrived almost immediately. I forwarded it on to the insurance agency and included a note to call Bret Singer because the claims adjuster would need the entry code to the marina. Then I called Marinette's police department.

"Scott St. Germain here. I need to speak to Detective Cole Dominic."

"Hey, Scott! How's it hanging?" Cole answered on the first buzz to his extension. He was always laughing or joking.

"Just wanted to give you a heads up on a problem at the marina last night." I related my story and asked whether Cole could check it out.

Detective Dominic and I have become close friends over the past ten years. He's studying for the bar exam, and I'm helping him prepare. Or, at least, I think I am. We were also partners on the Madison PD before I became an attorney and moved to Marinette. Cole transferred to Marinette PD last year to get away from the big city and an ex-wife named Candy, who was a total mental case.

"Simone, please get Digger on the phone for me. I'll be out in the garage. I want to check if anyone has screwed with my Jeep. I'll be back shortly."

A couple minutes later I returned and Simone handed me the phone as I was giving her a thumbs-up in reference to the Jeep. My sporty new Wrangler was untouched by graffiti.

"Good morning, Digger. I hope I'm not calling at a bad time. I need you to listen to the gossip at the bars in our area. Maybe learn if anyone is mouthing off about spray-painting a boat at the marina."

"Yours?" he asked pleasantly

"Yeah, mine. And you don't need to sound so cheerful about it."

Digger laughed. "Do you think we ought to use your dog K9 on it?"

"Really funny, Digger! I'll pay for your time, but whatever you drink at the bars is on your own tab."

"Not a problem, boss. I'll start on it tonight. I'll let you know if I hear anything," Digger said and hung up.

Why would anybody want to do this? The question nagged at me. Who in the hell had I pissed off? They were questions that I really didn't have answers for.

Maybe it was a prank or a gang initiation. Yet, I was fairly sure it didn't have anything to do with a gang. We just don't normally have that kind of a problem around here. There are some drugs and bar fights that have taken place, but even those are quite isolated. When a gang-banger drug dealer appears in town, he stands out like a sore thumb. The cops would be checking them out immediately and would hustle them out of town, with a not-so-gentle nudge.

I called Cole again. "Would you like to join Simone and me for lunch at The Crew's Quarters? About an hour?" He accepted, as he always did.

The manager, Carl Levin, met us at the door. "Good afternoon, Scott. Would you like your usual table? The one next to the window that overlooks the bay?"

"Yes, I would, Carl. Thank you." Simone and I had just been seated when Cole arrived. I waved, caught his attention, and motioned him over.

"Hi, guys," he said taking his seat.

The waitress asked for our drink orders and left.

Simone turned to me. "Why do you refer to your yacht as a boat?" she asked, her eyes wide with interest. "That Viking Sports Cruiser is fifty-six feet long! The interior rivals the finest hotel suites I've ever seen. I pulled up all the details on my computer. It's powered by a Volvo D9-500 Diesel inboard too." She hesitated for a moment, thoughtfully unfolding her napkin and placing it on her lap. "I've been thinking. You've asked me aboard only once, but it seemed like the biggest yacht in the marina. You keep it in dry dock during the winter. And you use it just a few times a year... so why did you buy it?"

"First of all, it is a boat. A luxurious boat, but it's still a boat. And I didn't buy it," I answered. "I won it in a high stakes poker game."

Cole leaned forward, interested. "You won it?"

"Yes, I did. Fair and square."

"Tell me how that happened," Simone said.

"Well, about a year ago, I was invited to a poker game at the home of a very rich client by the name of Claude Curry. I represented him in a hostile takeover of his manufacturing firm. He had a couple of his wealthy friends there, and one was from Chicago. His nickname was Mo."

Cole nodded. "I think I know part of this, but not the full story."

"As the evening wore on I was slightly ahead in winnings. Then I was dealt a royal flush. That's the best poker hand a player could ever dream of. The betting escalated between me and the man from out of town. The other three players folded and dropped out. I knew I couldn't be beat, so I bet $50,000 with a personal check."

Simone gasped. "Fifty thousand!" she whispered.

"Well, the other man didn't have that amount with him or a checkbook, so he asked me if I'd accept his yacht named the *Snow Flake* as payment. The host verified that the *Snow Flake* was valued at over ten times that figure. I agreed to the offer. We turned our cards over at the same time. He had a straight flush to the king. That's the second best hand in poker. When he saw my hand, his eyes bulged as though they were going to pop out and roll across the table."

"What happened then?" Cole asked.

"He reached into his pocket, took out the keys to the yacht, and tossed them in my direction. 'I'll get my personal stuff and it'll be yours in the morning. I'll send you the title when I get back home,' Mo told me."

"You're one cool player," Cole said, admiration in his voice.

I shook my head. "I paid for the plane tickets for Mo, his wife, and the yacht crew to fly back to Chicago. The title arrived two days later. I've never played poker since."

"That is one hell of a story," Cole said. "Do you think it has anything to do with the yacht getting spray-painted?"

"I doubt it. That was over a year ago."

"Probably a dead end but I'll check out the previous owner's information," Cole said.

Lunch arrived and we were finished talking business. The food at The Crew's Quarters is that good.

3

Early the next morning I was halfway through shaving when the phone rang. Simone had the day off so I let it go to the recorder. When I had finished my daily grooming routine, I went downstairs to the office and checked for messages. There was only the one; it was from Cole asking me to call him back as soon as possible.

"Hey, Cole. It's Scott. What's up?"

"Scott, I have some information on your boat... that is, uh, your yacht. I was able to get the state Certificate of Registration and hull number from the database in Milwaukee. The department's known as the DNR, the Wisconsin Department of Natural Resources. Who'd a-thought? I traced it back to the guy you got it from in

Illinois. He's a pretty unsavory character from Chicago, by the name of Mike O'Bannon with the nickname of 'Mo'. He's been arrested several times, but he's like Teflon—nothing seems to stick. Most of his arrests involve distribution of cocaine. Suppose that's why the yacht is named the *Snow Flake?"*

"That's a very good possibility. I'll call Claude. Maybe he can shed more light on Mo."

On the second ring, Mrs. Curry answered. "Hello?" She sounded rushed, nearly in a panic.

"Good morning, Mrs. Curry. It's Scott St. Germain. May I speak to Claude?"

"Oh, my God! I thought you were the police calling," she explained. "I just got off the phone with them. I found Claude about fifteen minutes ago in our garage. There's a deep cut on his neck and a lot of blood. I think he's dead." Her voice choked with emotion.

Why the hell didn't she call 911, I wondered, but didn't say anything. "I'm on my way, don't touch anything and don't talk to the authorities until I get there." I hurried my words but tried to keep my voice soft and calm. I'd never met Mrs. Curry face to face. She wasn't there the night we played poker, or at least she didn't make her presence known.

I arrived at her house just as a police cruiser was pulling into the driveway. As I got out of my Jeep, one of the cops put his hands out in front of him as if he was going to stop me. "Police! Crime Scene Investigation—please do not come any closer."

"I'm the Currys' attorney. I must to speak with Mrs. Curry immediately!" I insisted, raising my voice over the squawking of a police scanner.

"Follow me, but don't enter the residence," the officer said. "I'll have her come to you."

At the same time, Cole was just driving up in his private vehicle. "Hey, Scott! What're you doing here?"

"Mrs. Curry and I spoke a few minutes ago. You know they're my clients. I wanted to be here if she needs me."

"I was in my truck when it came over the scanner," Cole said.

Mrs. Curry stepped out onto the porch. I could see she was quite distraught.

"May I speak to her here on the porch?" I asked.

"That'll be fine," Cole said. "I'm going to join the others."

She looked so frail; she was barely five feet tall. I put my arm around her shoulders and led her to one of the two chairs on the porch. We both sat down.

Two more police units pulled up. Three units plus Cole's vehicle—that was a lot of attention for a small town like Marinette. The officers were busy with crime scene tape and dusting for prints.

I held Mrs. Curry's hand. "Are you able to tell me what happened?"

"Last night I took a sleeping aid. For the last few nights I haven't been able to get a good rest. When I came downstairs this morning I couldn't find Claude. I thought perhaps he'd gone out to the garage—to feed our dog." She dabbed at her eyes with a tissue. "Then I found him lying on the garage floor surrounded by a lot of blood, and I called 911. And then you called, Mr. St. Germain." Her eyes were brimming with tears.

"Will you be okay if I talk with the police for a minute?"

She nodded.

I called Cole on his cell phone. "Hey, buddy. Can you join us on the front porch?" Turning and walking away from Mrs. Curry, I asked him, "What have you got Cole?"

"A murder," Cole told me. "Mr. Curry's throat was cut by someone who knew what he was doing. No sign of a weapon. The coroner is on his way. Maybe we can get an approximate time of death. I'm calling in the state police for help. This is beyond our department's capabilities."

"Okay, no need to come out here now. Here's what Mrs. Curry has told me." I related what she'd said. "Is there any reason you'll need to question her further?"

"No, not at this time. Maybe later."

"I'm taking her to a friend's house. If you need to talk with her later.... Just remember, I insist on being present," I said.

"Would you please ask them to lock the house up when they leave," Mrs. Curry asked as we were getting into my Jeep.

I walked back to the crime scene and relayed her request.

"Will do," Cole said. "I'll call you later."

After delivering her to her friend's house it was four thirty in the afternoon. I headed for the The Crew's Quarters: I needed a drink.

Since the dinner crowd hadn't arrived yet, I took my favorite table, and Cole was still busy at the crime scene. It was one of the few times it was quiet enough in the restaurant that I could hear any conversation in the whole place.

A lovely and shapely lady was just walking in. She took a seat at the bar and ordered a gin and tonic. Several minutes later, I heard her ask the bartender: "Who's the handsome, Tom Selleck look-alike over there? Minus the mustache, of course." She gestured toward my table.

"That's Scott St. Germain," the bartender said.

"What kind of work is he in?" She continued, "Is he married?"

"He's a local attorney." The bartender was busy polishing glasses. "No wife that I know of," he replied.

She left a ten-spot on the counter, picked up her drink, and walked over to my table. "Hello. My name is Kory Sims. May I join you?"

I stood and offered her a seat. "My name is Scott St. Germain. Do we know each other Ms. Sims?" I said and we both sat down.

"No, Mr. St. Germain, we do not."

"Please, Scott will do."

"Call me Kory." She smiled, a warm gorgeous smile. "The bartender told me you're an attorney here in Marinette."

"Yes, as a matter of fact, I am. Are you in need of legal counsel?"

"Maybe. What sort of law do you practice?"

I hesitated a moment. "I think it'd be easier if I told you what law I prefer not to engage in."

"And that is...?"

"I don't take cases involving real estate, corporate law, or estate planning," I answered. "If I may ask, what kind of work do you do, Kory?"

"I'm an author."

"That's where I've heard your name before. I believe I've read some of your books."

Again, she smiled that gorgeous smile. "Did you enjoy them?"

"It's been awhile, but I believe I did. I'm sure at least two of your books are in my library. May I buy you another drink?"

"That sounds delightful—if you'll have another, that is," she responded.

The dinner crowd had begun to trickle in, and the

noise level was escalating. I pulled my chair closer to hear over the clamor. "Are you new in town or just visiting?"

"Actually my grandfather lives here. He's quite ill. My parents were killed by some guy trying to carjack them in Chicago ten years ago. I've come here to make arrangements for Papa to go into an assisted living facility. Do you possibly have any recommendations?"

"As a matter of fact, I do. There is a location called The Royal Palms."

"Gads! It sounds like a seedy motel in Miami."

I laughed. "Kory, I assure you that it's not. I'm sorry about your parents."

"Thank you. I'll check out The Royal Palms for Papa tomorrow."

"I know you didn't come to my table to ask me about assisted living. What's really on your mind?"

"You're right." She leaned in closer to me too. "I'm starting a new novel and, oddly enough, the lead character is an attorney. I've never written about this subject before.... I know I'll need a bit of help about the law and courtroom procedures."

"I'm certain I can help you with almost any question—concerning the law—that you come up with. Since you're new in town, perhaps I could show you around."

"That would be fun. You're not married?"

"I married once, right out of high school. A year

later she was killed in an automobile accident."

"I'm sorry for your loss too," Kory said.

"Thanks for your concern, but it was a long time ago.... Are you? That is, are you married, Kory?"

"No, never married," she said softly. "And right now there's no one special either."

"Here's my proposed fee agreement. I'll charge you one date for each legal question you ask me. Does that sound like a deal?" I asked. This was quite unlike me, but I was enjoying the moment.

Kory's answer was another rewarding smile. "Yes, I believe it is."

"Very well. Here's my card, but in exchange, I'd like a number where I can reach you." My phone buzzed annoyingly in my pocket. "Excuse me, I have to take this." It was Digger. I covered my other ear so I could hear him better.

"I need to meet with you, boss. I've got news on the spray-painting," Digger told me.

"I'm finishing up some business. I'll meet you at the house in an hour," I shouted over the mounting noise of the dinner crowd.

"Fine, I'll be there." We both hung up, and I put the phone back in my pocket. "Where do you call home, Kory?"

"Sheboygan, Wisconsin. Have you ever been there?"

"No, I haven't. What's it close to?"

"The city is about seventy-five miles south of Green Bay. Just a few hours drive from here, right on Lake Michigan. You must come visit sometime."

"Sorry I've got to cut this short. Business to attend to, you know."

"I understand. I'll be expecting your call," she said.

Reluctantly, I took my leave of The Crew's Quarters and the lovely Kory Sims.

4

Digger was right on time. I met him at the front door, and we walked back to my office. "Okay, let's hear it," I said and sat down at my desk.

"Well, after I had visited several bars I decided to go over to Little John's pool room." Digger sprawled out in the chair across from me. "I hadn't been there five minutes and I heard this guy spoutin' off about spray-painting an ol' boat in the Marinette Marina. I also heard a couple guys call him 'Punky.' So I waited outside until he came out and got into his car. I copied the license number. The name Punky is unusual, so I'm guessing it was a nickname—like mine." He handed me a scrap of paper where he'd written Punky's license number.

"You got a description?"

"Yeah. Thirty or so. Five-ten and maybe about one seventy-five. Clean shaven head and dirty clothes. Has a tattoo of two teardrops below his left eye."

Hmm.... He certainly sounds like a punk to me. "Thanks, Digger. What do I owe you?"

"Um.... One C-note should cover it. I was only out there a few hours. Hope that helps, boss." He pushed back his chair, stood, and left.

I called Cole and it went to message. "I have information concerning my boat's mishap," and then proceeded to relate Digger's story. "Check him out and let me know when you have something."

~

In Chicago, Mike O'Bannon's throwaway phone buzzed and he answered it. "Yeah?"

"The first part of the job is done," the voice on the other end of the connection said. "I'll complete the second part soon." The caller hung up and was gone.

Mo glanced back at the hallway mirror, studying his reflection. "That will teach those bastards to play me for a fool," he muttered and raised a plump fist. He was convinced that Claude Curry and Scott St. Germain had conspired to fleece him out of a large sum of his money the night the attorney took his yacht the

Snow Flake from him. Whoever heard of a royal flush and a straight flush to the king in the same hand? The chances of that would be a trillion-to-one.

Mo had just spoken with Manny Bruso. Manny was a low-life thug whom he had used for a hit man in the past. Mo had personally driven Manny to Menominee to show him where Claude Curry lived, then they went back to Marinette and checked out the residence of Scott St. Germain.

"I've made new fake ID and Illinois driver's license for you," Mo was saying as they drove. "It's in the name of Samuel Smith. You'll need them for renting a car and a few other transactions. Here's a down payment for the job." He'd handed Manny a briefcase with the IDs and $50,000 in cash.

Manny was a man of few words. "Looks right," he said.

"You'll get the other half when the job's done." Mo drove Manny to the car rental agency, dropped him off, and headed back to Chicago.

Mo had several legitimate businesses to hide behind while he made his real money trafficking in cocaine. One was an automobile dealership, and the other was a string of fast food restaurants. He was in poor health, suffering with Type II diabetes, was extremely overweight, and his cocaine habit didn't help his health in the least. However, if anyone screwed with Mo, he would either get a payback or he would be eliminated.

My phone buzzed. The text read: "Scott, come to PD. ASAP."

I arrived at the Marinette police station minutes later, one of the benefits of living in a small town.

"I've got him in an interview room. You can watch and listen at the one-way glass," Cole said before entering. "Punky, my name is Detective Dominic. I need you to tell me about the spray-painting job you did on a yacht in the Marinette marina."

"What do you mean? 'I did'!" Punky shouted, his anxious voice spilling out into the hall where I was waiting and watching.

"I've got surveillance camera shots of you doing your work."

"I didn't see any cameras," he said and scratched at his shaved head.

"So you admit you were there."

"Ah... well, yeah. I guess, if you got the pictures."

"What I really want to know is why you did it?"

"Don't know. Just for kicks, I guess."

"Bullshit, I've got you on breaking and entering, and defacing of personal property. With your past criminal history, you could be doing some time." Cole slapped Punky's file shut. "I could make that all go away, if you come clean with me."

"Okay, I was paid to do it."

"How much?"

"A thousand bucks for ten minutes work."

"Who paid you?"

"Sam."

"Sam?" Cole repeated.

"I don't know his real name, just some guy who told me to call him Sam."

"Start from the beginning." Cole said patiently.

"I was playing pool at Little John's, when this guy challenged me to a game. He said he would spot me three balls, and give me ten-to-one odds he could beat me. I play a pretty good stick, so I slapped down ten bucks. Figured it would be an easy hundred to me. He let me break and then he ran the table. He wanted to know if I wanted to earn the money back I had just lost, plus more for just a few minutes work."

Cole said nothing, waiting and calm.

"Well, I said, 'Sure.' Then he told me what he wanted me to do. He drove me to the marina, and I sprayed the boat like he asked. I was suspicious of him, so when he dropped me off I copied down his license number," Punky said.

"Give me the plate number then get the hell out of here," Cole said.

Punky handed over a scrap of paper where he'd written the plate number.

"Can I still keep the thousand bucks?" he asked.

"One more thing, Punky," Cole said. "I need a description of this guy Sam."

"Okay. Let me think now.... Maybe about six-one. Dark hair that's receding. Late forties, I'd guess, and really bad teeth. He's got this scar that runs from ear to under his nose on the left side of his face." Punky leaned back against the sagging plastic chair, arms folded across his chest.

I watched Cole frown at this almost too perfect description.

"Is he a big guy? A small guy?"

Punky tilted his head, as if he hadn't understood the question.

"Any idea how big he is—how much he might weigh?"

"One-eighty." Punky's answer was almost too glib, too fast.

"That yacht belongs to a local attorney. You may want to pay him for the cost of getting the paint off," Cole said.

"I will if you'll drop the charges—and if it doesn't cost over a thousand dollars." Punky was pleading, wringing his hands.

"He's right outside. I'll let him deal with you directly," Cole said.

"Okay, fine. I'll do dat,"

"Mr. St. Germain, would you please come in?"

I pushed open the door and stepped inside, into the

stale, acrid atmosphere that all interrogation rooms always seem to have no matter where they are.

"Hello, Punky. My name is Scott. I've spoken with the marina maintenance shop about the paint. They told me they have a liquid solvent that will take the paint off without harming the exterior finish of the boat's hull. If you're willing to do the work, I'll forget this ever happened. What do you say?"

"Yeah, sure. I'll clean it up for ya'," Punky said.

"Fine, I'll meet you at the marina entrance in an hour and you can start working."

Punky was waiting for me when I arrived at the marina. The work was completed in less than thirty minutes, and Punky was on his merry way, with a cool grand still in his pocket.

Meanwhile, Cole had run the plate number Punky had given him; it came back to a car rental business. The information on the rental agreement turned out to be bogus and a total dead end. The rental service said they had already cleaned the car and rented it again a few hours later. Sam, or whoever he was, was now in the wind.

Something about this stinks; the whole mess was nagging at me. Who in the hell was this "Sam"? Where did he come from? He wasn't from around here if he'd needed to rent a car.

There were absolutely no clues concerning the murder at the Curry household. No one could find any motive, weapon, or evidence. The state police had quickly ruled out the small and frail Mrs. Curry as a suspect.

The residents of Marinette and surrounding area were becoming uneasy. Both the local newspaper and radio station were hard pressed to find anything else newsworthy to talk about in a small market like Marinette and Menominee. And rather than being helpful, they were creating fear among the residents. Most of the local folks were avid hunters; each of them owned several weapons. People who had never locked their doors before were now taking extra precautions. It seemed that wherever anyone went—to the market, to a restaurant, or to a bar—killing was the topic everyone was discussing. Of course, each person had his or her own idea of who had done it.

Mystery man Manny Bruso was renting a room at the Dodge Inn Motel in Menominee, using the alias Samuel Smith. He was taking his time, waiting for the heat to cool down before completing the second part of his assignment.

There was a knock on the door; he reached for his gun. "Who is it?" he asked.

"It's the manager, Mr. Smith. I wanted to tell you that we're having a party this evening for all our guests. It's at the pool," the manager said. "The motel is furnishing everything. Hope we'll see you there."

"I can't make it." Sam hesitated a moment. "I'm not feeling well."

"Is there anything I can get for you?"

"No thanks. I'll be all right."

Sam settled back against the pillows and turned down the volume on the television.

5

That day I decided to call Kory, and she picked up on the second ring.

"Hi, Scott," she answered. Of course, her phone would show who was calling.

"Hey, Kory. I was wondering if you'd have time this weekend to go for a cruise on my… uh… my yacht," I said.

"You have a yacht?"

"Well… I call it a boat but others refer to it as a yacht."

"Sounds like fun, how should I dress?"

"Causal, I guess. But bring a bathing suit if you want to. Never know if we might take a dip or lie on the deck and get some sun."

"Is this a date? If it is, you owe me a legal question," she said.

"Well, I think you would call it a date. So I owe you. Is Sunday morning about nine okay?"

"I'll be ready," she replied. "My granddad's place is 115 Raymond."

"I know exactly where the house is. I have a fishing buddy who lives across the street at 112 Raymond. Go to your front window and peek out. Tell me if you can see a beat-up, old green Buick in the driveway."

"Yes, as a matter of fact I do see it," she said.

"I'll see you at nine on Sunday."

My mind was busy with ideas of where we would cruise and what to do on Sunday. Tomorrow I'd go by the marina, tidy up the boat, and get ready for our trip.

Sunday morning at seven I was finishing my breakfast when my cell phone buzzed; the display showed it was Cole.

"I wanted to let you know, I located the rental car our mysterious Sam was using. My guys are dusting it for prints now. I know we will come up with several and I intend on running them all." He sounded mighty satisfied with the progress.

"Thanks, for the heads-up, Cole. I'll be out on the water most of the day. I have a date with a new lady.

I'm not sure if I'll be able get cell reception where we're headed. Leave any updates on my business number. I'll check on them when we get back."

"Will do. Have fun now," Cole said and clicked off.

I pulled up to her address on Raymond Road. Kory was watching from the front window and she waved to me. When she came out the side door of the house I could see that she was carrying a small gym bag and wearing light blue shorts, a white cotton blouse, and deck shoes. She looked wonderful. I got out of the car and opened her door.

"Thank you, sir." She greeted me with that fantastic smile.

"You're very welcome, my lady." I smiled too.

We drove to the marina, walked out onto the dock where my yacht was tied up, and stepped aboard.

Kory appeared awestruck. She looked around, momentarily speechless.

"Let me show you around," I said.

"Oh, my! This is beautiful." She stepped down the ladder into the main cabin and gazed around. She sat for a moment, testing the plush cushions that covered every surface in the salon and moving from one place to the other. The former owner had decorated his yacht with lavish taste.

We stepped up the ladder onto the aft deck and continued up one more level.

"This is the bridge." I said.

She reached out, lightly touching the vast array of electronics that were arranged all around and set in gleaming teakwood. "It's marvelous.... What's this?" She was pointing to a flashing LED light.

"Oh, that's a police scanner," I replied. "I have one at home and another in my Jeep."

She laughed. "You're not an ambulance chaser, are you?"

"No, but I am a first responder. I've been certified in several life-saving courses. You never know when you'll be called on in an emergency."

We continued the tour, viewing the galley, salon, and the sleeping quarters.

Kory pointed to another set of doors nearer the bow. "And what's here?"

"That's what called the head." I laughed and tapped my forehead, trying to be funny.

"Don't be silly," she said. "I know what it means. It's good to know where the facilities are, though."

I grinned. "I have hereby appointed you my first mate and with that comes duties."

"Oh, indeed? And what do the duties entail?" Kory seemed genuinely puzzled.

"You will cast off the bow lines and stern mooring lines. Then you'll take bumpers off and store them. After that you are free of duties until we dock again."

"Aye, aye! I can handle that, Captain." She tossed off a remarkably good salute.

I slowly maneuvered the craft out of the harbor, obeying the speed limits on the marker buoys, and out into the bay. I plotted our course, entered it into the computer set for ESE, and we were underway.

The water was smooth, with only a few ripples caused by a light breeze from the south. Above us there was plenty of blue sky and an occasional white puffy cloud. I couldn't have asked for better weather if I had custom ordered it myself.

Kory had changed into her swimming suit and was unrolling her mat on the upper deck. "Would you mind if I get some early morning sun?" she asked.

"No, not at all." I took a longer look than was absolutely necessary. I told myself I was making sure she was safe up there and wouldn't trip on any of the neatly looped lines or anything else. I couldn't help but think that she was one beautiful lady.

Our destination was across the bay, to a small port called Egg Harbor on the west side of the Door County peninsula. The distance across the bay to the harbor was nineteen miles, give or take, and I throttled back a bit. I wanted to take my time, enjoying the day with her.

"Tell me about the book you're writing, Kory." I was gazing down at her creamy golden shoulders and back. Her bikini didn't hide much, but she was lying on her stomach.

She turned to meet my eyes, her cleavage accentuated, exposed and so tempting. "It's a novel about an attorney who'll be defending this one woman. She's gotten herself mixed up with a bunch of guys that were committing bank robberies. During the last robbery, a bank guard was killed." She paused before continuing. "I have eleven chapters completed so far. My books usually end up a minimum of fifty chapters—at least 80,000 words. That equates to around 350 pages or so in print."

"Are you staying in Marinette long enough to complete it?"

"I'd like to stay for the rest of the summer and make sure Papa is doing okay."

"I hope you'll need lots of help with legal advice, at least a dozen times before the summer ends." I didn't even try to disguise the hope in my voice.

"I'm sure I'll have a lot of questions by then." She smiled, stood up, and fastened her bikini top before I had a chance to glimpse more.

Back on the bridge, Kory came around to where I was seated and once more monitoring the computer settings at the helm. She came up behind me, put her arms around my neck, and gave me a light kiss on my cheek.

"This is a beautiful day. I'm happy to be spending it with you," she said.

Damn! How I wanted to kiss her back, but one small power craft towing skiers was crossing my wake and another was dead ahead. I couldn't turn away. "If you look straight ahead, you can see land. That's Egg Harbor. We're halfway there."

"I'm going below to change," Kory said.

"When you come back, could you bring us a couple of beers? Okay? They're in the fridge."

"Aye, aye! I'll be back in a few," she said and disappeared below deck.

The icy, cold beer went down real easy. It also helped cool me down.

An hour later, I was maneuvering the yacht into the marina and luckily found an empty slip. Kory tossed out the bumpers and secured the lines.

"All secured, Captain," she announced.

We walked up the dock to the harbor master's hut where I paid for a three-hour slip rental.

"Are you ready for lunch?"

"You bet," Kory said.

I took her hand and we strolled up and out of the marina. "I know this great restaurant with an outside patio. It's only a couple blocks away."

Today, especially on a Sunday, the little town was busy with tourists. The street was so jammed with car traffic that we easily made better time walking than we would have driving. We didn't have wheels there anyway.

After we'd finished lunch, Kory asked, "Do we have time to go shopping?"

"Absolutely," I assured her. "I want you to enjoy the day. Where would you like to begin?"

"I want to start on the right hand side of the street, go up maybe two blocks, and then come back down the other side. As busy as it is, I think that it'd take us about two hours. Does that sound right?" Kory's pretty baby blues gazed up into my eyes, as if she were asking for the greatest treat she'd ever had.

The shops along the street all had unique items ranging from souvenirs to nice but inexpensive jewelry. Kory had showed a special interest in a beautiful multi-colored cloisonné ring. "This is beautiful," she said. She studied it for several minutes, but then told the clerk, "Maybe I'll come back later."

We continued visiting each store taking notice of what they had to offer and were nearly finished. Kory was carrying an armful of purchases she was sure she couldn't live without. I wanted to go back to the shop that had the ring she'd liked so much, but I didn't want her to know what I was doing.

"I'm going over to the ice cream shop to get a cone. Would you like one?"

"Sure!" Kory said. "Make mine chocolate."

I hurried back to the shop, purchased the ring for her, shoved it in my pocket, rushed to the local ice cream parlor, and returned with our two cones. I figured I'd give her the ring later, maybe with a friend-ship card. Our time was up when we reached the boat slip, and minutes later we were heading out into the bay on our way back to Marinette.

I pushed the throttle forward, increasing speed, and the boat responded instantly. Soon we were cruising at near maximum speed. "Would you like to take over?" I asked, gesturing toward the control panel. "This is the power throttle. Forward—increases speed. Pull back—and it slows the boat. The wheel is just like on a car. You can turn right or left." I showed her where the power throttle was located and explained the basics of the instrument panel, although I always felt like I was aboard a star ship. The previous owner had made certain every possible gauge, gadget, and instrument was installed, from sonar and radar to engine boosters.

Then I settled back in the captain's chair and enjoyed watching as she stood at the helm. With the breeze and the motion of the boat blowing her hair back, she was smiling and appeared to be enjoying herself.

"Kory, how's your papa?"

"As well as you would expect for a man in his eighties and in poor health. I made sure that a neighbor would check on him while I was gone today. Oh.... I visited that place you recommended, The Royal Palms. I was pleasantly surprised."

"Let's slow down," I said. "We'll try for a reasonably slow speed. That way we won't endanger other recreational boaters." I set the computer to resume our heading back to the marina. I wanted to spend more time with her.

We talked about everything and nothing at all. It seemed we both expected much of the same things from life. I was pleasantly surprised: I hadn't felt this comfortable sharing with a woman in many years. When I was with her, the lingering memory of the grisly execution was starting to fade.

Two hours later we were back at the Marinette marina. After securing the lines on the yacht, we climbed into my Jeep and headed for her grandfather's home. It had been such a pleasant day I didn't want it to end; I hoped Kory felt the same.

"Would you like to top off the day with dinner at The Crew's Quarters later this evening?"

"I'd love it," Kory said. "Give me time to check on Papa, shower, and get changed."

"Sounds great! I'll pick you up at seven."

All was well when I arrived home. There were three messages on the recorder but this was Sunday, and I was certain they could wait.

Nearing seven o'clock I turned the corner onto Raymond Road. Ahead, the street was full of flashing red and blue lights. An ambulance and two police units were parked in front of Kory's place. I thought immediately of her grandfather.

I parked and approached the officers. "What's happened?"

"There was a 911 call from an old man who said his granddaughter had just been beaten."

I turned and started for the front door.

The officer grabbed me. "You can't go in there."

"The hell, I can't. I'm her attorney." I pushed the cop aside. Once inside, I saw Kory on a gurney; she was terribly battered. I reached out and touched her hand. "Kory, it's Scott. You'll be okay, sweetie. I'll make sure you get the best care."

"Move aside, please, sir," one of the paramedics was saying. "We need to load her in now."

The older man, whom I assumed was her grandfather, was being treated with oxygen while a cop was getting his statement about what had taken place.

I went outside where many of the neighbors had gathered. "Excuse me, folks. Does anyone here know who looks in on Mr. Sims when Kory is away?"

One lady stepped forward hesitantly. "I'm Lee Balsis," she said. "My husband Joe takes care of him when it's needed."

"Would you mind helping just for now? Until we can arrange for some professional staff to be here?"

She nodded. After checking with the police, she

went back inside the house to ask how Kory's grandfather was doing.

This time I *was* an ambulance chaser. I followed their speeding vehicle to the emergency entrance at Marinette General Hospital. I helped with the necessary paperwork the best I could. "Sorry," I told the admissions clerk, "That's the best I can do for now. We'll fill in the blanks later."

I sat in the emergency room waiting area until Kory was admitted. The little flower shop in the hallway had closed for the day. All I would have to offer her, when I saw her, was a big smile.

When I finally was allowed to see her, one of the nurses met me at the door to her room. "I've already given Miss Sims a sedative to help relax and ease the discomfort. It should be wearing off in about a half-hour."

That was good, I thought. I could use that time to check with the PD.

I phoned Cole, and my call went voice message as usually did. "Hey, Cole. Please check into the report call on Raymond Road, about seven this evening. Give me a call back. The victim is my lady friend." I paused a moment before adding. "No, I wasn't the one who beat her up."

Time in a hospital always passes slowly. I was waiting for any response from Kory. Her right eye was black and blue and had already swollen badly despite the ice packs. Her lower lip was split; it was twice its normal size. A large bruise covered her right cheek. I sure would like to get my hands on the son of a bitch who did this to her.

She began moaning and tried to open her left eye.

"Kory, it's me, Scott. You're safe now. We're in Marinette General Hospital."

"Is Papa okay?" she managed to whisper.

"Yes, he's doing fine. The neighbors are with him."

"Good." She turned her head into the pillows.

"Can you tell me what happened?" I asked.

"Could I have a drink of water first?" she asked. "My throat is so dry it's hard to swallow. I hurt like hell."

"I'll bet you do," I said. I held a plastic cup of water close, the straw bent to make it easier for her.

After several small sips of water her voice became stronger. "What do I look like?"

"I'll get you a mirror in a minute. But the way you look now, I don't think you'd want the picture on the back cover of your next book."

Kory tried to grin, but her pained expression warned me not to kid around anymore.

My phone buzzed and I answered. "Hey, Cole. Glad you called back."

"I'm outside Kory's room," Cole said. "Is it okay to come in?"

"Let me ask her." I covered the phone. "Do you mind having a visitor?"

"I don't suppose so," she said, but it sounded like it had been an effort for her to speak.

"Sure, she's awake now," I said. "Come on in."

Cole stepped in, all broad, muscular six feet of him filling the doorway.

"Kory, this is a very good friend of mine. Cole Dominic is a detective here in Marinette."

"Nice to meet you Miss Sims," Cole said. "Wish it were under different circumstances."

"Nice to meet you too," Kory answered, trying to smile.

"I've talked with your grandfather, about the incident at his home today. He told me that two men forced their way into the house when you answered the door. Is that correct?"

Kory nodded, but then grasped her head. Every movement must hurt something terrible.

"Do you know these men or did you recognize them?"

Again, Kory nodded, but held her head while she did.

"What happened next?" Cole asked.

"They begin screaming at me. They called me disgusting, filthy names. Then they pushed me back inside." Kory paused and sipped at the glass of water I was holding for her. She took a deep breath and winced at the pain. "Papa must have heard the commotion from his bedroom. He came to help me. When they saw him, one of the men pushed Papa down. They threatened him with his own cane. The other man was hitting me in the face and kept on calling me a bitch, a whore, a slut… lots of other vile names. After he was done using me as a punching bag, they left… and I called 911." Kory was exhausted from speaking.

"I checked with the doc," Cole said. "He said you have a broken nose, lots of bruises and contusions, and a split lip. You'll probably have a black eye for a while, but he says that within a week you should look better and feel a lot better. Do you want to press charges on these guys?"

"You're damn right I do. And on the guy who sent them to beat me up."

Cole and I shared a quizzical look. I shrugged. "And who may that be, Kory?"

"Bernie Sandowski. The other guys are Gabe and Vinnie Rollins—they're brothers. Vinnie is the one who beat me. They all live in Sheboygan."

"How do you know Bernie Sandowski?" Cole asked.

"I had been dating him for a couple of months. Then I broke it off last month because he had gotten weird and possessive."

Cole was writing in the little notebook he always carried. "Had he ever hit you before?"

"No. Never. But he did pin me against the wall a few times—he was in a rage that frightened me. I didn't need that in my life." Kory paused to swallow with an effort. "I told him I never wanted to see him again. He was cursing me as he stormed out the door. That happened over a month ago, and I haven't seen him since."

"He must have been keeping track of you all that time." Cole was completing his notes.

"Kory?" I laid my hand on hers. "If this goes to court, do you want me to represent you as your attorney?"

"Yes, Scott. That would make me very happy."

Next week would be Claude Curry's funeral, and I would pay my respects. I knew also that Cole would be there discreetly in the background, hoping to get a glimpse of someone that seemed out of place. Why did funerals always seem to take place on rainy days, adding to any onlooker's already saddened state of mind?

The people would be around the grave, their umbrellas held close to shield them from the rain. It would be hard to identify anyone. It hardly mattered, because I was certain the killer would not be in attendance. It was just a gut feeling I had.

6

It had been a week now since Kory's assault. Both the Rollins brothers were in jail awaiting trial. However, Bernie Sandowski was a different matter. He had a slick lawyer who had managed to keep him from being arrested and put in jail.

This did not sit well with me at all. Once in a while, I've considered that a person needs to have friends in the right places for special problems. And occasionally I've been fortunate to have those friends. I called on Digger, who had a friend, who had a friend, who had two friends who were retired after a number of years with the NFL. They worked now and then to help certain people acquire a "new understanding" of leaving a person alone. I finally heard that Mr. Sandowski was in

ICU. He'd had an accident; it seems that he tripped and fell. Strange how that happened. I'm sure he got the message, and I didn't ask any questions. The Rollins brothers would have their court date and would be found guilty. The prosecutor was going for a minimum six months in jail and would be ordered to pay Kory's hospital expenses.

Manny Bruso was developing a raging case of cabin fever. He had isolated himself in the motel room for too many days, more than he could count, and was getting tired of having his meals delivered by fast food businesses. The four drab walls of the motel were closing in on him. He snatched up the phone book and called a cab.

"Take me to the nearest gin joint," he told the driver.

Minutes later they pulled up in front of the Interstate Lounge. Manny paid the cabby and went inside. There was a small crowd, but it was early evening. The juke box was playing softly, and a couple was making out on the small dance floor, pressing close to each other like they were about to have sex.

Manny didn't want to draw any attention to himself, so he took a seat in a booth at the back of the bar. A couple of drinks later, he noticed there wasn't anyone using the pool table. He'd always shot a good game, and many times he'd hustled guys out of their paychecks. He started playing alone, deliberately missing easy shots. In case anyone was watching him, he didn't want to look really good. It wasn't long before a big man walked up to the pool table.

"You live around here?" the man asked in a deep voice.

"No. Just visiting a friend," Manny answered.

"Would you like to shoot a couple of games with me?" the big guy asked.

Manny shrugged. "Sure, why not?"

"How about playing—say, ten bucks a game?"

"Wow," Manny said. "You must be pretty good."

"Okay, rack 'em up."

The first two games Manny lost on purpose. He wanted the other man to think he had a fish on the line.

"Increase it to twenty bucks a game? Okay with you?"

Manny played the unwilling and wronged player. "I guess that's the only way I'll get my money back," he said reluctantly. He went on to win the next four games. "Four in the side pocket." *Clack!* "Two in the right corner and six in the left." *Clack!*

The big man was breathing heavily, his jaws clenched and his fists bunched at his side. He'd already crushed one chalk cube in anger. "I'll raise the bet again."

Manny raised his hand, a gentle calming gesture. "Tell ya' what. I'll play you just one more game. That's it. Stakes are for everything you've got in your wallet."

The man laid $400 on the table.

The action around the table had attracted several bar patrons. Manny matched his bet. They decided to break on a coin toss. Manny won. He broke and promptly proceeded to run the table. The big man never got in even one shot.

The big guy lunged at Manny in a fury and grabbed him by his collar. "You're a damn hustler! I want my money back."

"No fuckin' way," Manny said calmly and stepped back.

The big man charged at him again. Manny crashed the pool cue across his face. Blood spurted from the man's nose as he fell to the floor. After two more quick whacks to the back of the man's head, Manny was sure he wouldn't be getting up any time soon.

Someone in the bar yelled, "Call the cops!"

Manny didn't want anything to do with the cops and sprinted out the back door, headed for the peace and quiet of his motel room. Out of breath, he lay on his bed panting. His evening out hadn't gone the way he thought it would, but at least he'd returned with over $500 in winnings.

When the cops arrived at the bar, the patrons gave them a physical description of Manny: A little over six foot, slender, dark hair, and a big scar on the right side of his face. No one knew his name or had ever seen him before. The big man had a broken nose and a hell of a headache. The cops treated it as just another bar fight.

When Kory was discharged from the hospital, I drove over to pick her up. Other than the purplish discoloration under her left eye she looked fine.

"I've decided to take Papa to Royal Palms Assisted Living," she told me. "I'd really like to get him settled in."

"Sounds like a wise idea," I said. "You know, for your own safety you can stay at my place for a few days. I've got lots of extra bedrooms."

"Scott, that's sweet of you. I'll take you up on your offer."

"I'll try my best to be a perfect gentleman." Even though I would love to get next to her, I knew her life was in turmoil. If I rushed her, it would add to her problems and might very well ruin our relationship.

Kory arrived back late that afternoon and parked her car behind the house.

The next morning I went to the kitchen and made a nice breakfast for her. I *can* cook when I have the incentive and produced a reasonably nice omelet. I surrounded it with slices of sourdough toast and two pieces of bacon. There was even a glass of fresh orange juice and a cup of coffee. I dashed out to the garden, picked whatever flower was growing there and stuck it in a small glass, and then started upstairs with the tray.

Simone was at her desk and noticed. "What's going on?" she asked.

"We have a house guest for a few days," I told her and continued on my way upstairs.

"I need to talk with you for a minute," she said.

"Okay, I'll be right back," I called over my shoulder. I knocked softly on Kory's door. "Breakfast!" I said.

"Slide it under the door." She sounded sleepy.

I laughed. "I can't do that. It won't fit."

"I can't let you see me this way in the morning," she said.

"Okay. I'll leave it by the door, but don't let it get cold." I went back downstairs to my office.

"I assume it's a lady guest that's upstairs," Simone whispered.

"Why would you assume that?" I asked.

"I just don't think you're the type that'd be making a nice breakfast for a man."

"You're right, Simone. Her name is Kory Sims. And she's a friend."

"Is she the author? *The* Kory Sims?"

"Yes, one and the same. Have you ever read any of her books?

"Yes, as a matter of fact. I just finished one I found in your library," Simone said.

"Now what are the questions you have for me?"

"I need to pay several fairly large bills. You'll need to transfer money into the business account. Otherwise I'll be writing out checks that won't clear."

I nodded. "All right. What else?"

"I'd like to announce that K9 has been successfully trained. He goes to the back door and yaps to be let out when it's time for him to do his business. He's a good little fellow."

"You're kidding." I shook my head. Simone always managed to surprise me. "How'd you do that?"

"Boss, never mind now. You need to do *your* business and get some cash flow back into the accounts."

Simone had a way of letting me know when it was time to buckle down. She was right. There were two past due cases that were still not completely paid off by my clients. I called them both and reminded them of their tardiness. They each assured me that the check would be in the mail tomorrow. We've all heard that line before. I remembered when I was a horny teenager and telling a girl, "Just let me put the head in." I knew that was a bunch of bull crap and so did she. However, I'd be watching closely to see whether they'd follow through with their promise to pay.

7

Cole called and explained that his ex-wife Candy was IN town. "She wants to see me," he said. He'd stalled her until later in the afternoon.

From what I could remember Candy was a stone-cold bitch, always after a way to make some easy money. I had been around them back when Cole and I were cops in Madison; that was when they were first married. Judging by some of the crap she pulled, his buddies—like me—could only conclude she was certifiably crazy.

We'd made an appointment to meet at my place before he met with her. When he arrived, we went into the kitchen, and I closed the door for privacy.

"Okay, Cole, what is it she wants?"

"That bitch wants more alimony. She told me, if she doesn't get it she will take me back to court and make my life a living hell."

In my opinion, she'd already done that, but I didn't say anything. "What's changed in her life that she suddenly feels the need for more money?"

"She told me she's buying a new house and with her current income she won't be able to qualify for the loan," Cole said.

"Has she retained an attorney?"

"I have no idea."

"Well, you know I'll represent you if it comes to that, and I won't charge you. However, you will owe me a due bill."

"Let's hope it doesn't come to that." Cole seemed more glum by the minute.

"Is she here alone?"

"As far as I know."

"Where and what time are you meeting her?"

"Three o'clock at Burgers & More on Main Street."

"I'll call Digger and have him check out what she's driving and where she goes after your meeting. As your attorney, I'm advising you not to agree to any thing she suggests. Just tell her you'll let her know later."

"She won't like that much." Cole pushed back the chair at the kitchen table and stood up. Our short meeting was over. "I'll check in with you later," he said as he left.

Digger arrived at Burgers & More fifteen minutes before Cole's scheduled meeting and chose a parking spot that gave him a full view of whoever drove in or out of the parking lot.

Cole was exactly on time and went directly into the restaurant. A few minutes later a super-sized pickup truck pulled into the lot. It was jacked up much higher than a normal truck and had extra large tires, adding even more height to it. There were two people inside.

The passenger side door opened, and a woman was attempting to get out. Her short skirt was so tight she was hiking it up as she tried to reach the running board and again when she stepped down to the ground. Digger shook his head. This gal was something to behold. Her hair-do was all spiked up, and she wore too much heavy makeup. How did she possibly manage in those stiletto heels? At one glance he could tell she wasn't from around their area.

The driver appeared to be quite a large man, but he stayed in the vehicle. To make certain she was the one Cole was waiting for, Digger decided to enter the restaurant a few moments after her. The same woman was seated with Cole in a booth. He waited at the front counter for a waitress to take his order for a coffee to go. Behind him, Candy was pounding her fist on the table and making a scene. Her voice was loud, and she sounded angry.

After the waitress handed Digger his coffee, he turned and gave the spiked-hair woman one last look and then left for the security of his car. Minutes later he had finished the coffee, and Candy came walking across the parking lot. Again, she struggled to climb back into the big truck.

Traffic was light. Digger didn't have any trouble keeping an eye on the big truck. Following behind at a discreet distance, he watched the truck turn into a motel at the edge of town. Digger pulled over to the curb and called Cole.

Cole answered on the first ring. "What've you got, Digger?"

"Your ex is booked in at the Big Beaver Lodge on Route 41. Do you know where it's located?"

"Yeah, I know exactly where it is." Cole added it to his notebook.

"I've got the plate number. It's Wisconsin FIS4FUN. A big, yellow Ford 250 jacked up so high you'd get a hernia just getting in the damn thing," Digger said.

"I'll let the guys on patrol know and see if they can find probable cause to pull it over. I'll have them run wants and warrants on the vehicle and the driver. We'll see if anything comes up. I appreciate your help, Digger. Now I gotta call Scott and let him know how the meeting with my ex went down," Cole said and hung up.

Cole returned to his office for the remainder of the afternoon, so much on his mind he found it difficult to concentrate.

"Dominic!" A voice boomed from the front of the squad room. "Line 2. Some guy named Less Fuller."

"Hello, this is Cole Dominic. How may I help you, Mr. Fuller?"

"Mr. Dominic, I represent Midwest Mortgage Company. I'm calling in regards to the loan application a Ms. Candace Dominic has given us. She has indicated that you will be giving her $20,000 as a non-repayable gift and an increase in her alimony of $500 a month. Is that correct, Mr. Dominic?"

"No, that is not correct Mr. Fuller!" Cole was seething but made a note of Fuller's phone number. The area code didn't seem to match up. "I have no intentions of giving her anything. There will be no increase in the alimony. Period. I met with her today, and I can assure you that there was never any discussion about a monetary gift—of any amount—and it will not happen now or in the future."

"Thank you, Mr. Dominic," Less Fuller said and hung up.

Cole forced his attention back to the more urgent matter of the jacked-up Ford. His computer showed the vehicle in question had several citations that were overdue for appearance. The owner of the vehicle had two outstanding warrants. A Jerald Wozniak was listed as the registered owner. The warrants were for assault on a police officer and carrying an unregistered fire arm.

He called over to one of the uniforms. "Don, you and your partner go sit on this guy and wait until he pulls onto a city street. Then pull him over and arrest him. Be careful. He may be armed. If there's a woman in the truck with him and her name is Candy Dominic, just let her twist in the wind." Cole smiled, feeling the bitterness of years past coming back. What had he ever seen in Candy? He shook his head.

8

After Claude's funeral service, a long line of cars followed the hearse to a cemetery outside of town. A respectable-sized crowd had gathered at the grave site and the pastor was saying the final words. I knew Cole was nearby watching everyone. I wondered, as I always did, whether the killer was among us.

When it was over I spotted Cole and walked over to him. "Anything new on this case?"

"No, not a damn thing." He was watching the people getting into their cars. "How is Mrs. Curry?"

"Not too bad," I said. "Her kids have arrived from out of state and have been helping her. Have you heard from your ex again?"

"No. All is quiet."

"Let's hope it stays that way. I'm going to head back to my place and check on Kory. I'll see you later, Cole."

I walked in the back door and found Kory at the dinning room table, typing feverishly on her laptop. She was so engrossed in her work that I startled her.

"Damn, you nearly scared the pee out of me." She looked up at me through her bruises that were somewhat improved.

"I'm sorry," I said. "Are you working on your book?"

"Yes. With everything's that's happened, I've fallen behind on my schedule. I believe it's time to go back to my grandfather's place. I have some catching up to do," she said. "And there's his house.... There's just so much to do."

"Kory, I have an idea. You gather up what you've brought here, and I'll load your car. That way we'll have time for an early dinner at The Crew's Quarters. Afterwards, we can come back here and pick up your car. Then I'll follow you to your granddad's place."

"I'd love that, Scott. You're always such a gentleman."

Yeah. I know, I thought, *and that's probably why I'm not getting any place with you.*

It was five thirty when we arrived. There were plenty of tables available, and since it was a weekday we would have our choice. "Could you seat us over there by the last window?" I asked the waitress. "We'd like a nice quiet place to enjoy our meal."

"It would be my pleasure, Mr. St. Germain." She picked up two menus and led us to the table.

I pulled out a chair for Kory and adjusted it when she'd sat down. A few minutes went by while we perused the menu, studying the list of entrées.

"I'll have the baked salmon," Kory said.

"I'll order the oysters on a half shell first," I announced after a moment's more study. "Then for the main course, the broiled trout for my entrée."

Kory winked at me from across the table.

Had she read my mind, thinking that the oysters were an aphrodisiac—although that was nothing but a myth—and that I had something else on my mind? Well, I did.

The waitress returned. "Would you like a glass of wine?"

"Hmm....Would you like to order a bottle?"

Kory nodded enthusiastically. "That'd be nice, Scott."

"Please bring us a bottle of the Pinot Grigio." The waitress smiled and left. Moments later she appeared and poured a small amount in my glass. The regular procedure of sniffing and tasting wasn't really needed with this particular wine. I nodded my approval. It was light and refreshing, a perfect end to our day. Our waitress poured for each of us.

"Let's toast to our friendship," Kory said and raised her glass. "May we become even closer."

"I'll drink to that," I said. I hoped it was an invitation to take the next step.

Our meal was served. The broiled trout at The Crew's Quarters is the best I've ever tasted, browned and seasoned just right. Kory seemed to like her selection too. Soon we were enjoying a second glass of wine.

"I'd love to go on another outing on your yacht." Kory held out her glass again. "Just a little bit, please."

"We should do just that. There's two months of summer left, and we should take advantage of them," I said. Soon we'd finished our meals and the wine.

In the lounge, there was a three-piece band that had started to play some soft dance music. Here was my chance to finally hold her in my arms.

"Would you be so kind to dance with me?"

Without hesitation she answered, "I'd be delighted."

I escorted her to the edge of the dance floor, faced her, and pulled her close to me. She laid her head on my shoulder as we moved to the music. Her body felt warm and her perfume was pleasantly intoxicating, not so strong that it was overpowering, but as if it was a part of her.

"It feels so good to be held again," she said.

"The feeling is mutual," I whispered in her ear.

After our second dance, she said softly, "You need to take me home."

So that was it. I was wondering how we'd gotten our signals crossed as I paid the check. We left, and Kory was quiet on the drive back. We picked up her car and drove to her grandfather's place.

"Please come in." Surprising me, her words were soft as a kitten's purr.

"You go ahead. I'll grab your bags and computer from the back seat."

She left the door ajar and disappeared down the hallway. "Just put that stuff on the kitchen table," she called. "I'll be out in a few minutes. See if you can find any romantic music on the radio."

So her old grandfather didn't have any modern devices, just a standard old radio. I switched it to FM. Lo and behold, there was a selection of mood music.

"Scott?" Kory called back to me. "Could you please close the blinds and turn the lights off in the front room? There's wine in the fridge, I think. Open it and pour us a glass. I'll be out shortly."

After pouring the two glasses of wine, I turned off the kitchen light and took a seat on the sofa in the living room. The hall was still lit, the light from the other end reflecting dimly into her living room. Moments later, Kory stepped out wearing a filmy gown, the light behind her revealing a perfect outline of her body. She was naked. My heart was beating faster, and there was a rush filling my entire body. She sat down beside me and placed her hand on my thigh.

"What do you think?" She moved even closer and her lips brushed mine, a gentle promise of a kiss.

"My mother told me that if I ever had impure thoughts, I would turn to stone. I think I've already started." I was breathless, but I was trying to make a joke anyway.

She laughed as we sipped our wine.

"Did I break the spell?" I asked softly.

"Not at all." She drew me closer, and at last, we kissed a long, long time, a deep and passionate kiss. She must want me as much as I wanted her.

We finished our wine—which I probably hadn't needed—because Kory's kiss was intoxicating enough. She took my hand, leading me to a bedroom at the back of her house. Together, we lay down on the queen-sized bed, never breaking contact, while she undressed me and I took off what little she was wearing.

Then we were exploring each other's body, wildly, with total abandon. I certainly felt up to the task ahead; it had been along dry spell for me. She slid down my body until her mouth covered all of me, giving me pure, crazy, and wonderful pleasure.

Then it was my turn. I started by kissing her beautiful breasts, going from one to the other, until her nipples became large and firm against my tongue. Then Kory's hands were pressing on my head. "Hmm?" I asked, my mouth still on one delightful breast. It was the left one, I think.

"Oh, yes.... Please." She increased the pressure on my head.

When I arrived I noticed she was clean shaven and wet with anticipation. I buried my face between her legs and discovered she tasted absolutely wonderful too.

"Come on, big boy," she whispered. "I want you deep inside me."

Later I would try recall every moment of that night. I'd tossed aside the sheets and come up to her. Her legs were parted, waiting for me, and I'd plunged deep inside her. She was soft, slick, and everything about her seemed to welcome me, just me.

After we'd made love for the first time, we lay together savoring the intimacy we'd just shared. Her hand rested across my chest, and she was murmuring something sweet. That would be the time we both would have lit a cigarette, I thought with some amusement, but neither of us smoked.

Several hours later—and after making love again, more gently and tenderly—I decided I should go home. We kissed, and I dressed slowly and reluctantly. Kory walked me to the door.

"I'll call you tomorrow," I said before I kissed her again. Although I didn't want to go, I left.

It was eight thirty in the next morning, and I had just finished shaving when the phone rang. It was Cole. "Hey, Cole!"

"Just thought I'd let you know we picked up Mr. Wozniak and impounded his truck. He's in a holding cell. My ex-wife was left at curbside throwing a hissy fit. I think she went back to their motel room. She's called here twice but the operators told her I was out and they would take a message." Cole chuckled. "And each time the phone went dead."

"Between the news of Mr. Fuller and her boyfriend being put in jail, her day isn't going too well."

"Be careful, Cole, that woman is off her rocker." I wanted to warn him; I was always cautious around crazy people.

"Will you have any time available later this evening?" Cole asked.

"Sure. What do you need?"

"Some help on my law studies."

"Not a problem," I answered. I was surprised he'd have time right now. "Come on over after you finish work."

9

At Manny Bruso's motel, the cell phone buzzed; the display showed it was his boss in Chicago.

"Yeah, Mo?"

"I'm sending a guy up with a delivery for you. It's a five-pound package of cocaine. I want you to plant it on that yacht, somewhere in the engine compartment. Then you're to call the DEA with your burner phone and tip them off about the cocaine on the yacht. I want that prick of an attorney to suffer."

Manny heard the anger building in Mike O'Bannon's voice.

"I'm going to have you turn his world upside down before he's put to sleep permanently," Mo continued. "The guy I'm sending up there's going to leave you a new car. You won't have to use rentals any longer. He'll take the bus back to Chicago. Meet him tomorrow at the bus station in Marinette at 3:02 p.m. He'll be driving a black 2013 Ford Mustang. He answers to the name 'Snake.' Got that?" Mo asked.

"Yeah, boss. Sure thing," Manny answered.

Manny arrived at the bus terminal at quarter to three and watched the car traffic pulling in and out. At exactly three o'clock a black Ford Mustang pulled in and parked two spaces away from him.

"Snake?" Manny said.

"Yeah. Are you Manny?"

"In the flesh. You got something for me?"

"It's in the trunk. Keys are in the ignition. See you around." Snake spoke quickly and then disappeared back into the bus terminal.

Manny drove to the marina where the *Snow Flake* was docked. He walked around to where he could read the names on the sterns of all the various boats.

And there it was. The *Snow Flake* was second from the end on B dock. Finding it was child's play. He pulled out his phone and typed in "nearest scuba shop." That, too, proved easy to find. He followed the directions and parked at the store.

"May I help you?" the man behind the counter asked.

"Do you have any kind of waterproof bag that could handle objects—say, up to the size of a shoe box?" Manny asked the store clerk.

"Sure do. Will this do the trick?" He held up a medium-sized, vinyl bag with a shoulder strap. "Do you plan on diving around here?"

"No. It's a birthday gift for a friend," Manny said. "I'll take it."

"That's $35.50. Would you like it wrapped?"

"Nah. I can take care of that." Manny slapped the cash down on the counter and left, his purchase tucked under his arm.

Later that evening Manny drove to the far end of the marina and waited until dark. He had brought a bath towel from the motel. The half-moon gave him just enough light to guide him to where he was going. He stepped out of his shoes and removed his socks. He walked down the grassy bank to the edge of the water; there he stripped off his clothes down to his under-shorts. He placed the shoulder strap of the waterproof bag with its contents over his head and waded sound-lessly into the cool water. He'd already decided that the breast stroke would be best for avoiding any sounds of splashing that might alert the guard in the marina office. By the light from the dock lamps he could easily read the names on the sterns.

He was treading water quietly and listening for anyone close by. He made his way along the yacht to the front and hoisted himself up and onto the dock. Crouching down he walked to where he could step aboard the *Snow Flake.* After a few minutes he found the hatch to the engine compartment, opened it, stepped inside, and closed the hatch behind him. He reached into the waterproof bag and brought out the flashlight. He looked around; the space was quite small. Shining the beam around he finally found the metal box mounted on the hull marked "Emergency Flares." He unfastened the straps that held the box securely and studied its contents. Manny removed the eight flares and replaced them with the five-pound bag of cocaine. He dropped the flares in his bag—he wasn't sure what else to do with them. Last, he secured the box to its proper location.

Manny reversed his course until he was back to where he started. Grabbing the towel, he dried himself, got dressed, and returned to his car. He picked up his burner phone and dialed a number.

Mo answered on the first ring.

"The package is in place," Manny said and hung up.

Manny was pulling into the motel parking lot just as the manager was walking by.

"Hello, Mr. Smith." The manager greeted him with a friendly smile. "Did you buy a new car?"

"Yeah. Just picked it up today."

"It's real sporty," the manager said. "I'll change the information on your registration. Illinois plates, you know. Good night, now." He continued walking to the motel office.

"Damn it all," Manny muttered.

Back in his room, Manny dialed out on his burner phone.

"DEA, Green Bay Station," a woman answered.

"I want to tip you guys off about a yacht named *Snow Flake* in the marina in Marinette, Wisconsin. There's a good probability there's cocaine aboard."

"Who's calling please?" the woman continued politely and automatically.

Manny switched off.

At the DEA office in Green Bay, the agency's operator stared down at the phone that had just gone silent in her hand. She entered the phone number in the computer database and within seconds it had come back as an untraceable burner phone. Still the DEA operator relayed the message to the senior agent in charge, Brad Conley.

"Thanks, Mona. We'll check it out. Nine times out of ten it's bogus—just someone pissed at someone else. Abe, check out a watercraft registered as the *Snow Flake* in Marinette and give me the owner's name and address," Conley said.

Conley's assistant entered the data into his computer. "The boat's last known docking location is the Marinette Marina. The owner's name is Scott St. Germain, and his address is 51 N. Riverside Drive, Marinette, Wisconsin," Abe Crawford read from the computer screen."

"Okay, gentleman. I want four of you to pay Mr. St. Germain a visit, but *only* after I receive a specific search warrant from a judge," Conley directed.

A few hours later the four agents were on their way to Marinette.

10

I had just returned from the supermarket and was putting away my groceries. There was a knock at the front door, and K9 rushed toward it in a frenzy of barking. The large, oval, stained glass panel made whoever was outside look fuzzy and out of focus, but I could tell there were several people waiting there. I scooped up the squirmy, yapping bundle of dog and opened the door.

One of the men shoved his foot inside the door, blocking any attempt I might have made to close it. Another pushed K9 and me to one side. A third man handed me a neatly folded, crisp document. I recognized what it was but didn't want to believe it.

The leader of the group showed his badge and

leaned in close to my face. "We have a legal warrant to search your home and any and all outbuildings, all your vehicles, and your boat."

I was totally taken by surprise and by their rush to enter. "See here. I'm an attorney and I want to know what you're searching for." I made every effort to sound both polite and stern. I did know my rights. K9 started trembling again. I put him down and he scurried away upstairs and to safety.

"Read the warrant, counselor," one of the men said.

"'Cocaine and/or related paraphernalia.'" I read out loud. "But that's ridiculous. I need to watch as you search."

"Fine with us," one officer said.

"I need each of your names and your agency," I demanded.

The lead officer stopped what he was doing and took out a note pad from his vest pocket, wrote down the information I requested, and handed it to me.

Back when I was a police officer I had executed several warrants myself. This was the first time I had ever been on the receiving end; it was not a pleasant experience.

After finishing with my house, they went to the garage and dug through the Jeep and the RV. Next we went to the marina and boarded my yacht. About twenty minutes later, I heard one of them calling from the engine compartment.

"Over here!" the officer announced.

We all gathered around. He was holding a strange, lumpy package, something I'd never seen before.

"Test it, John," the lead man said.

The man who discovered the package took it out to the galley, where there was more space. He laid it on the galley counter and carefully used his knife to cut a small hole in the package. A small stream of white powder leaked out. They used the DEA's field test kit, and the powder immediately turned blue.

"That's a positive," the agent said.

"Mr. St. Germain, you are under arrest for the possession of cocaine with the intent to sell."

He proceeded to read me my rights. I must say he had Miranda down pat. I nodded, then recalled that I had to actually say that I understood what he'd said. They instructed me to put my arms behind my back and placed handcuffs on my wrists. The package of cocaine was sealed tight in double evidence bags.

"Would one of you please drive my Jeep back to my home before taking me to jail?" I asked. "The keys are in my right pocket."

"Sure, Mr. St. Germain," one of the men said. He looked like he felt a bit sorry for me or maybe like he couldn't believe what had just happened either.

The man in charge of the DEA detail produced his badge and ID at the Marinette Police Station. "We're requesting that Mr. St. Germain be held here until further notice. We'll be in touch," he said and handed them his card.

We walked through the hallway until we came to a holding cell. Several of the police officers I passed were clearly puzzled. They knew who I was and were likely wondering why I was in cuffs. No one said anything, but word got to Cole almost immediately. When the DEA guys left, Cole appeared at my cell.

"What the hell's going on," he asked?

"They found a large package of cocaine on my boat," I exclaimed. "It was in the box for our emergency flares."

"Is it yours?" Cole asked.

"Of course not," I answered.

"Where are your flares?"

"Hell," I said. "They didn't give me time to look or ask."

"Did anyone take prints?"

I groaned. "Probably not."

"Where in the hell did it come from?"

"Beats me." I shook my head. Nothing made sense. Kory and I had just been out on the *Snow Flake*—she hadn't gone down near the engines.

"Do you think someone planted it there?"

"Either that… or it's been there since I took ownership of the boat," I said. "Can you call Digger? Have him come visit me."

"What else can I do to help?" Cole asked

"Go to 115 Raymond Road and tell Kory what has happened, maybe her ex-boyfriend is involved. Also call Paul Sheppard. He's my attorney."

"Sure thing, Scott. Anything else?"

"Yes. Would you stop any place and pick me up a hamburger—just anything? I'm starved."

"I'm on my way," Cole answered and left.

Digger arrived at the jail next. We talked in an interview room, a guard observing us from the other side of the one-way glass.

"Digger, check on those guys in Sheboygan, the ones that beat up Kory," I said. "See if they're dealing in cocaine or if they are trying to frame me," I said.

I really didn't think they were smart enough to put it together, but you never know. It seemed that the only other ways the drugs could have gotten on board were that they were left by Mo or planted by him. Cole had earlier told me that Mo had been suspected of dealing drugs.

"I'll probably be in Sheboygan for a few days." Digger wished me luck as he left.

Paul Sheppard arrived shortly after Digger, and I explained the whole story. "Could you go back to the marina and see what's going on?" I asked him. "In the entire year that I've owned the boat, I've never been down with the engines."

"Do you know if they dusted for prints?"

"No," I said. "Could you ask them to? Maybe something will show up. If any are found, they sure as hell won't be mine." Although I was feeling mighty sure of myself, I was also trying to recall whether the DEA agents were wearing gloves when they were poking around. I hoped to hell they had been.

I had been in the holding cell for only a short time and it was already becoming uncomfortable and oppressive. Then I thought about Kory.

~

Kory Sims was seated at her kitchen table, industriously typing on her laptop computer. Occasionally, she'd stop and made a note on a yellow legal pad. She'd been through this process before and knew what steps she must take to make her latest book a good read. For some reason thoughts and words weren't coming as easily as they'd usually come before. She stood up to stretch, hands above her head, and she worked through a series of exercises she'd learned that were always helpful to prevent cramps in her neck and shoulders. She strolled into the living room and gazed out the large front window.

There was an unfamiliar car across the street; it was parked in front of the house where Scott had told her that his fishing buddy lived. It was a black Ford Mustang with dark-tinted windows. It was impossible to see if there were any occupants inside. Kory sighed and stepped out onto the front porch; fresh air might help her think better. The Ford's engine roared to life, and the car quickly sped away. She wondered whether she should be concerned about the car; it seemed more than strange.

I'll mention it to Scott. Maybe his fishing friend drives a black Mustang. It was strange too that she hadn't heard from him. She returned inside and immersed herself in her work. It wasn't long before she'd forgotten all about the black Ford Mustang.

11

Finally, Paul Sheppard managed to have me released on bail. The judge ordered me to surrender my passport—I had to ask Simone to search for it in my files—and told me not to leave the state. Luckily, I had not taken on any other cases, which freed me to devote all my time to what was happening.

However, the DEA was still trying to build a case against me, even though they hadn't found my prints on the package of cocaine or anywhere else in the engine compartment. One set of prints they traced to one of my marine maintenance crew, the team that made sure that everything on the *Snow Flake* was kept in perfect, pristine, and meticulously working condition. Another set was a mystery: still no matches.

When they'd interviewed me in jail, I related the story of how I'd become the owner of the yacht and who the previous owner was. I gave them a brief summary of Mo's reputation.

I would learn later that the senior DEA agent had contacted the Chicago office, and he'd received an earful concerning Mike O'Bannon.

When I arrived home from our city jail, I called Digger. "Hey, pal. Do you have any contacts in Chicago?"

Digger was silent for a brief moment, probably going through that card file that all investigators carry around in their heads. "I have one close friend who works in that area," he finally answered. "However, my license isn't valid in Illinois."

"Could you contact him and tell him that you'll be coming to Chicago? I'd like to hire him to do a workup on Mike O'Bannon. You can work along side him, can't you?" I waited until Digger grunted his consent. "I want to know everything about that guy. Where he lives, what he does, where he goes, who his friends are, what he drives, and most of all if he's involved with cocaine. Stay there as long as it takes to complete the job."

"Can you afford this, boss?"

I laughed. "I've got to. Ask if your man has any friends in the Chicago's local office of the DEA. See what they have to say about Mo."

"I'll try to reach him this afternoon... see if he's available. You never know. He may be involved with another project," Digger said and then they hung up.

The phone rang again just as I had put the handset back in the cradle. The display showed it was Kory. *Oh, God!* Throughout this ordeal I still hadn't called her.

"Hey, sweetie. How're you doing?" I said automatically. I had a lot of explaining to do.

"I was going to ask you the same thing," she said.

"Oh, honey—" I began.

"It's okay. Cole just called me, about an hour ago. He wanted to know if—while I was on your boat—I had ever gone into the engine compartment. I told him I hadn't. I don't even know where it is." Kory's tone had turned cool. "What the hell was that all about?"

"Don't worry, honey. He's just trying to tie up lose ends."

"Lose ends to what?" she demanded.

"To why I was arrested."

"Arrested?" Kory exclaimed.

"Yes, let's have dinner tonight and...."

"I'm not sure. Maybe it's not a good idea. I have so much work to do... my deadlines—"

"Please?" I wanted to recapture the mood of our last dinner, if I still could. "I'll tell you the whole story. Can I pick you up at seven?"

She hesitated a moment. "Okay. I'll be ready. Oh! Scott, I wanted to tell—"

But I had already hung up. The other line was ringing and Simone had stepped out for a moment.

It was edging toward seven o'clock when my Jeep and I pulled into Kory's driveway.

I'd just opened my car door, but she had already come out the side door next to the driveway and was hopping in before I had a chance to get around and open her door.

"Hi, sweetie," I said.

"Hi, hon," she said. "You're right on time. I like that. Dependable and a man of your word, despite being thrown in jail."

Yes, I will have a lot of explaining to do. I put the car in reverse and backed out into the street.

"Damn, there it is again," she said as we started down the street.

"What is?"

"That black Ford Mustang we just passed."

"What about it?"

"There's something weird about it. I saw it earlier," she said. "I was going to tell you."

"I'll swing around the block and get the plate number."

Minutes later, when we arrived back at Kory's house, the car was nowhere in sight. Kory told me about when she'd first seen the car. I considered it a bit strange but probably nothing to worry about. My first thought was perhaps the DEA had put a tail on me.

As we were heading to dinner I explained to her why I'd been arrested and put in jail.

She looked concerned, pulling away from me a bit. "You're not into cocaine are you, Scott?"

"Certainly not!" I said emphatically. "You sound like you're not quite sure who I am."

"You're right, I guess. I shouldn't have asked. Now I'm sorry I did, but I do need to know, for my own safety." She leaned over and kissed me lightly on the cheek.

"Thanks. All is forgiven." However, I understood her hesitancy: all of us are judged by the company we keep. A few minutes later we pulled into the parking lot of The Coyote Moon Restaurant. I didn't want to face the familiar crowd at The Crew's Quarters.

The Coyote Moon was located on Highway 180 about three miles north of the city. They had opened recently, and I had heard good reviews about their food. Their specialty was seafood, and since it was Friday night I wanted to try their fish fry. Just about any place that served food or alcohol in our Twin Cities area had a fish fry every Friday. The parking area was almost full.

Entering the restaurant, we were greeted by a smiling young lady. "Welcome to The Coyote Moon. Do you folks have a reservation?"

"No, I'm afraid we don't," I said.

"We have seating at the bar. Will that be all right until a table is ready?"

"Sure," I said and Kory nodded too.

The young lady led us to two empty stools at the end of an intricately carved, ornate bar that was constructed of black cherry wood. I was impressed by the quality of the workmanship. The owner of the restaurant was making his way through the patrons' tables, stopping at each one and chatting with them.

He arrived where we were sitting, extended his hand, and introduced himself. "Good evening folks, I'm Kenneth Bentley—" He seemed to recognize one of us. "Oh! I believe I know you. Aren't you the fella' who has the yacht *Snow Flake* tied up at the marina?"

"Yes, that's correct. Have we met before, Mr. Bentley?" I shook his hand, wondering how he knew about my boat.

"Well, not officially. My yacht, the *Moon Beam,* is docked beside yours."

"I'm Scott St. Germain and this lovely lady is Kory Sims. She's a special friend of mine." I wanted to close the conversation before he asked any questions about the other day when the DEA boarded my boat.

The bartender appeared and asked for our drink order, which fortunately sent the owner off in another direction, introducing himself to new arrivals.

Bentley glanced back at me. "I need to talk with you later," he said softly.

I didn't want to seem like a jerk, so I grinned, waved, and gave him a thumbs-up.

We were sipping on our second drinks when the pretty young hostess came up to us. "Your table is ready now. Please follow me."

After we'd been seated, Kory asked to be excused. "I left my purse in the Jeep. Could I borrow your keys?"

"I'll be happy to retrieve it," I said.

"You're such a gentleman. But I can get it—I know right where it is. I'll be back in a jiff."

She was back in seconds. Her face was deathly pale.

"Scott, you need to come with me." She gulped and continued. "The parking lot was dimly lit, but I found your Jeep. Your windshield's been smashed in! I first thought I had come to the wrong car.... But I knew it was where you'd parked."

I was starting to get up, but she had collapsed into the chair beside me.

"I tried the key in the door lock. It worked," Kory said, her eyes wide with fright. "I reached in and grabbed my purse and locked the door again. I was frightened. As I was running back here, that same black Ford Mustang surged out in front of me. It nearly knocked me down. Then it sped away in the dark." She reached for the glass of water the hostess had placed on our table and drank the entire glass. "The plates are not from Wisconsin. That's all I was able to get—it starts with Q. It was too dusty." She started crying.

"Oh, I'm so sorry, sweetheart." I put my arm around her shoulder. "Are you okay?"

"Yes, just a little shaken, I guess."

"Let's get out of here," I said.

"But we haven't had dinner yet," she tried to protest.

On our way out, the owner Mr. Bentley came up to us. He looked concerned. "Is something wrong?"

I handed him my business card. "Call me. We need to talk," I said in as stern a voice as I could muster at the moment.

12

Driving, while peering through the shattered maze of my windshield's safety glass, was a challenge. The minute I got home after leaving Kory's place, I called the Sheriff's Department because the incident had happened outside the city limits. I hadn't wanted them to come to the restaurant and cause problems for Bentley or his customers, although it should have been documented at the scene. The person I talked with said they would send a deputy out in the morning to take pictures and get a statement from Kory.

Someone was screwing with me: first my boat, then me, and now my Jeep. That left my house and the RV. I needed someone to really check into this. But who? Digger would be out of town for who knew how long.

I'd call Cole and see if he could give me any off-duty time.

"I need your help, Cole," I said and laid out my predicament.

"Do you have a plan?" Cole asked

"All these attacks seem to be happening at night. You'll probably need to watch the house after dark. If I go out with Kory, shadow us. I'll pay you for your time, of course."

"I wouldn't think of charging you, Scott. Hell, you're giving me all those free hours helping me with my studies."

"Somehow I don't think the person who's messing with us will act again soon. There's a timeline between each of my 'mishaps'—if you can call them something that simple. But I also don't think they're finished."

"You're probably right. I'll wait two or three days and start then."

"Thanks, buddy," I said and clicked off.

Now I needed to call my car insurance agent and get started with that tedious process. If this person was trying to get under my skin, he was certainly succeeding.

The next morning I called Kory to see how she was doing. I felt terrible that our evening hadn't ended well. I was worried that her time here in Marinette had been full of too many unexpected problems and might cause her to go back to Sheboygan before the end of summer. I was becoming quite fond of the lovely Kory Sims, and I was fairly certain the feeling was mutual.

We made a date for dinner on Sunday at The Crew's Quarters. I was certain I knew exactly how to cheer her up. As a matter of fact, we'd both seemed more than cheered, but that night could have been months ago.

Manny Bruso lay on the bed in his motel room, drinking a beer, staring at the ceiling, and thinking. *I'll bet that scared the shit out of that bitch last night. Her boyfriend must have had one hell of a time seeing through his windshield as he drove her home.*

He laughed to himself. He was enjoying fucking with the guy and his girlfriend before he killed him. He laughed again and grinned as he opened another can of beer.

His burner phone rang and Manny answered. "Yeah?"

"Hi ya', Manny. It's Mo, how're things going up there?"

"Just doin' what you asked," he answered.

"Tell me about it," Mo asked.

"I put the package in place and made a call to the Feds. They checked his house, his car, the RV, and his boat. That's why they cuffed him and put him in jail overnight. He was out the next afternoon, then I checked out his girlfriend's house. When they went out to dinner last night, I fucked up his car and screwed with her in the parking lot. I'm sure he has no idea what the hell's going on. I think I'll do his house next."

Mo's dry chuckle came over the phone clearly. "Good work. How's the Claude Curry case doing?"

"It's been real quiet. I don't even see anything in the papers anymore. I think they're stumped," Manny said.

"That's the way I want it to be," Mo replied.

"Anything else you need me to do to this guy, St. Germain?"

"Yeah. Plant bugs in his house, car, and on the *Snow Flake*—so you can keep track of him. And maybe you could do his girlfriend just before you take care of him," Mo said. "That's always a nice touch, like a bonus."

"What do you mean by 'Do his girlfriend'?" Manny asked. Would he need to hang around here even longer?

"You know, take her against her will… whatever," Mo said. "Then kill her."

"Okay, I can handle that, but it'll cost you more money—a lot more than we agreed on."

"How about double?" Mo said.

"Sounds about right. Any particular way you want it done, boss?"

"Yeah. Make it grizzly, so the asshole will grieve. But I want him dead before the end of summer," Mo said and hung up.

On Sunday afternoon I arrived at Kory's house and parked in the driveway. I rang the bell on the side entrance.

"Come on in. The doors unlocked," she called to me.

She was on her cell phone with the manager of the Royal Palms. From the side of the conversation that I could hear, she was not happy.

"What was that about?" I asked.

"They called to tell me that Papa could no longer have a private room, because they're so many new people coming in. He's going to have a roommate, although their rates are remaining the same."

"When is this going to happen?" I asked.

"Tomorrow." Her voice was heavy with concern and disappointment.

"Well, let's head over there tomorrow. We'll see who his new roommate is and how he feels about it."

"I think that's a good idea…," she said. "Perhaps in the afternoon." We headed out the side door.

Tomorrow afternoon sounded like an excellent plan to me, because I was hoping she'd spend tonight at my place. We arrived at The Crew's Quarters at seven. The dinner crowd was still light, and my favorite table was waiting for us. Wanda, one of the waitresses I've known for years, took our orders.

Kory told her, "I'd like a gin and tonic, please."

"And for you, Mr. St. Germain?"

"I'd like a tall greyhound on the rocks," I said.

Wanda laughed and winked at me. "You didn't have your grapefruit this morning, I take it."

"That's about it," I said. Everything else in my life, including breakfast, seemed topsy-turvy right now too.

"Any appetizers?" Wanda asked.

Kory shook her head.

"No thanks," I said. "Not tonight."

I waited for Wanda to leave. "Kory?"

"Yes, Scott?"

"Before we order, there's something I'd like to give you." I reached into my coat pocket and pulled out the friendship card I'd bought while we were in Egg Harbor. I'd written a short note telling her how I felt about her. While she was reading my message, I placed the small ring box in front of her. Tears had formed in her eyes; they brimmed and then trailed slowly down her cheeks.

Kory opened the box and gasped. "It's that beautiful cloisonné ring I admired at the little shop in

Egg Harbor!" She dabbed at her tears. "Oh, Scott! You can't imagine how many times I wished I had bought this ring while we were still there." She leaned across our small table and gave me a long warm kiss. "Thank you so much, sweetheart," she said and we kissed again. "Can I stay the night?" Her voice was low, seductive.

"You must have read my mind." I looked deep into her eyes. Just the thought of having her warm, naked body next to mine had caused me to respond with an immediate erection. It would have been quite embarrassing, had I needed to stand up for any reason.

Kory must have known or guessed. She reached between my legs and squeezed me: I was as hard as a rock. "Let's not linger after dinner and head right for the bedroom," she said.

"Your wish is my deepest desire, my dear." I put my hand on hers under the table. If we planned on eating tonight, we'd better avoid any more caresses in the restaurant.

We drove home fast, in a happy expectant blur. We had barely made it upstairs before we'd stripped off all our clothes. For the next two hours we made passionate love. The night and everything about Kory had been exciting and wonderful. Alone in the bedroom, our problems were a million miles away.

"Hey, love? Could we go for another cruise on your boat?"

"My calendar's fairly clear. No new clients with new business right now." As I said this, I realized that I should be concerned about the bills, but at this moment I wasn't. "You could bring your laptop and work on your manuscript. We'll run up to Mackinac Island and make a three day trip out of it."

"Let's do it!" Kory exclaimed and wrapped her arms around me.

"I'll get the boat ready and stock it for the trip."

"We need to check on Papa before we leave," she reminded me.

"Of course. Then we can cruise up to Manistique and stop for the night. We'll spend the next night and day at Mackinac Island," I said. "The return trip will be one long day all the way back here."

"Scott, you're so wonderful. I'm so lucky to have you in my life."

"We do go well together, don't we?"

"We certainly do." In the dim light of a nearly full moon, I could see her smiling at me, tempting me. "I think we have time for a quickie, if you're up to it." She giggled and pressed my face against her breasts.

The next morning we showered together, slowly, enjoying ourselves. After we dressed, I drove her home. Reluctantly, I left her there and went my own way. I needed to prepare for our trip.

By two in the afternoon I was back at her house. We drove to the Royal Palms to check on her papa. He already had a new roommate.

"He never stops talking—even when he's alone," he told us. "That constant chatter is driving me nuts."

"Papa? Could we get you some earplugs?" Kory asked.

"My ears are just fine. It's my ticker that's giving me trouble, but I wish it was the other way around." he said with a grin.

Kory regarded him lovingly. "Papa, with all your problems, you still have a good sense of humor." She bent down and kissed him on the forehead. He smiled.

13

Kory and I had cleared the entrance of the Menominee River heading out into Green Bay, and the *Snow Flake* was purring softly against the gentle current. We were about to set our course when my cell phone buzzed. The display showed it was the senior DEA agent who had told me not to leave the state.

"I can't believe they're keeping such a close tab on me!" Exasperated, I sighed and answered. "Hello. Scott St. Germain."

The caller formally introduced himself first, as if my phone's caller ID hadn't been sufficient. "Mr. St. Germain, we wanted to tell you we've dropped our case against you. You are no longer under any restrictions, and you may continue your voyage out of state. We're pursuing another lead at this time. We're sorry for any inconvenience." And then he then hung up.

I couldn't believe it. They actually knew I was on the boat and headed out past the state line. But they'd dropped their charges. Suddenly I felt great, with Kory beside me on a totally beautiful day.

The weather on the water was perfect, with only a light breeze and a cloudless sky. I pushed the throttle ahead to near maximum speed, and we were on our way. About three miles out we skirted the shore line. There were few other craft out on the water today.

After a few hours, Kory went to the galley and made a plate of sandwiches. I cut back the engines to an idle. After checking the bottom with sonar, I set the electric winch before cutting the engines. It would lay out the sea anchor to keep the *Snow Flake* from drifting. After checking that the marker buoys were set properly, I joined Kory below; it was still brisk and cool on the aft deck. We ate lunch, which we accompanied with a can of icy cold beer.

"Have you ever heard of the Mile High Club?" I asked.

"I think so. Isn't that when you make love in an airplane when you're over a mile up in the sky?" She blushed or maybe it was from being out in the sun.

"That's correct," I answered. "I think we should make up a new club. Let's call it the Mile Out Club."

"What would that be?" she asked.

"Well... you'd have to be about mile out from shore and make love. We could be the very first members."

"I'm game."

She was laughing as we made our way forward to the master cabin. Shortly, the new club had been formed.

While Kory was getting dressed, I returned to the controls and set our course after making sure the sea anchor was reeled in correctly and stowed. Soon the Manistique harbor was in sight and we were pulling into a visitors slip. My first mate helped with the lines as she had at Egg Harbor.

Manistique is a small city in the Upper Peninsula of Michigan. The marina is also small but well maintained. I rented the slip for the night, since we planned to leave early the next morning. We decided to take a walk and return to the boat and eat dinner aboard.

"I want to show you that I can function in your galley," Kory said.

"How's the book coming?" I asked as we walked the streets of town.

"Actually it's doing quite well. The main character is just about to go on trial for bank robbery. That's where you'll come in, especially regarding courtroom procedures."

I laughed. "I owe you a *lot* of answers by now. Ask whenever and whatever you need."

Most of the homes in Manistique were at least one hundred years old, with broad, well manicured lawns and tall, lush trees throwing welcome shade across the sidewalks. The small downtown area was made up of old buildings housing retail shops of all descriptions that begged tourists to visit. We stopped for an ice cream cone.

"Just one scoop. I don't want you to spoil your appetite. I have something special planned for our dinner."

Kory wagged her finger at me as if I were a naughty boy. She was very special and I felt my feelings growing stronger for her every day.

We were walking back to the marina parking lot when a car with dark-tinted windows sped past us.

She spun around and stared after it. "I can't believe it. That's the same black Mustang!"

"Come on, sweetie," I said. "I'm sure there's a lot of black Ford Mustangs."

"Not with an Illinois plate starting with the letter Q!"

"Did you get any other part of the plate?"

"No. I was mostly looking at the car." She sounded frustrated and disappointed.

"I really don't think it's the same car. How in the heck would anyone know we were in Manistique? We're a hundred miles from home." I said.

We continued on to the yacht; nothing aboard seemed amiss. Kory went about preparing dinner without saying much; I could tell the incident was troubling her.

I found a CD that offered a selection of soft instrumental music. Then I set the table while Kory finished cooking dinner. It smelled delicious.

"Scott? Could you uncork a bottle of Fumé Blanc?" she asked. "I'm making Sole Meunière. The wine's light and should go nicely with the fish."

Now, I may not be the world's greatest gourmet, but I did know that Sole Meuinère was a classic French dish that I'd always loved, whenever I could order it. I'd already glimpsed the dessert she'd prepared: a Paris-Brest. The circle of puff pastry was filled with whipped cream and chilling in the galley's fridge.

Everything was extremely good—the meal was great. There was no doubt she knew what she was doing; she was a much better cook than I ever hoped to be. After we'd finished dinner, I poured another glass of wine for us, finishing the bottle.

We walked up to the main deck and settled into the two plush leather chairs mounted there. Above us, the night sky was filled with millions of stars. The water was so still it was like a mirror, reflecting the stars and doubling their light. I could not have custom-ordered such a romantic evening.

I set my glass down on the deck and reached for her hand. It was soft and warm in mine.

"Kory, I feel very serious about our relationship," I said, hesitating. "I hope that doesn't scare you off."

"Scott, it certainly doesn't scare me, because I feel

the same." She was staring up into the night sky. "But let's take it slowly, all right?"

"I agree." I squeezed her hand. At least she hadn't turned me down. We kissed and walked slowly back to the master cabin. I watched her as she prepared for bed, beginning to think about what it would be like if Kory and I were to marry. A quite nice, pleasant and warm feeling, washed over me. *Scott,* I told myself, *you are definitely falling in love.*

Several minutes later she slipped between the sheets and snuggled up close to me. Her scent was intoxicating. We made love, warm exciting love, again and again, until we both fell asleep, happy and exhausted.

14

In the morning, we went ashore for breakfast and hurried back to start the second day of our trip. Again, the weather was cooperating. I hugged the shoreline, so we could take in the beautiful scenery and rock formations.

Late that afternoon we cruised under the Mackinac Bridge at its highest point that connects lower Michigan to Michigan's Upper Peninsula. Mackinac Island lay five miles ahead. When we arrived, the island marina was nearly full. As we slowly cruised along the rows of boats, I spotted one that was pulling out of a slip large enough to handle mine. I idled until the other vessel had cleared and then pulled into the vacant slip.

After we had finished tying up, we walked up the

dock to where I would pay the slip rental fee. It seemed that every boat there was having a party, almost as if it were Mardi Gras time. There were a few young ladies parading around on their boats without their bikini tops.

"What kind of place is this anyway?" Kory asked.

"It's a very touristy place, but I don't think you'll find this type of behavior ashore."

The sidewalks and streets were crowded with people walking shoulder to shoulder or riding bicycles.

There were various ways to see the island and the historic landmarks. We decided to take a horse-drawn surrey. As we traveled around the island, the driver explained each point of interest as we passed.

When we drove by the Grand Hotel, the guide was announcing, "This is where the movie *Somewhere in Time* was filmed." It was a magnificent, gracious old building surrounded by lawns and flower gardens in full bloom. "No automobiles are allowed here except for the island's fire trucks and ambulances. The only way to get around—for tourists and the few full time residents—is by horse or bicycle. Our island is also famous for its fudge makers."

We decided to buy a pound or so when we arrived back downtown. Our ride took us past many stately old homes that overlooked the water. All the estates were well-kept and manicured. An hour later we arrived back where we'd started in the crowded town center.

The commercial part of the island extended for two blocks, with various retail shops on both sides of the street. There was a fudge shop about every third store. We found a place that looked promising and bought two pounds of mixed white and brown fudge. The funny thing was, neither of us liked sweets or candy.

It was dinner time and the driver of the surrey had recommended The Yankee Rebel Tavern as a popular island restaurant. Kory ordered the fresh white fish, while I had the mussels and Shrimp Diablo. We enjoyed a nice bottle of wine during dinner and finally retired to the yacht for a night cap. The party boats were quiet now, and we would be able to get a good night's sleep before starting for home tomorrow.

The next morning Kory fixed breakfast while I tidied up the cabin. We left the boat slip at six and headed for the fuel dock located at the end of the Mackinac Bridge in Saint Ignace, just five miles away. It was going to be a long day, but I figured we could make it home by five in the afternoon.

Manny Bruso had siphoned a gallon of gas from his car into a can and stashed it in the trunk of his car. He waited until three o'clock the next morning and drove to the street directly behind the house where Scott St.

Germain lived. The neighborhood was asleep; there was no traffic in sight.

Manny parked and left his car, carrying the gas can, flashlight, and rags around to the garage where St. Germain kept his RV. He protected his hand by wrapping it in a rag and knocked out a side window, the glass shattering inward without a sound. Reaching in, he placed the gas can carefully on a bench in the garage and then crawled in behind it. He opened the door to the RV, stepped in, and started splashing the gas around, first in the back and then worked his way forward, making sure the inside was well doused. Outside, behind the RV, he used the flashlight to help locate a shovel. After breaking out the rear window, he wound the rest of the rags around the shovel handle, lit them on fire, and tossed the entire shovel into the RV. The interior erupted in flames.

Manny slipped out through the side door of the garage, raced back to his car, and sped away.

Cole had noticed the flames reflecting from the neighbors' windows. He jumped from his car and dashed up the driveway, dialing 911 on his cell phone as he ran. The fire trucks arrived within minutes and were able to put out the blaze quickly.

"The structure has some damage, but it looks like it might be repairable," one of the firemen told him. "However, between the fire and water damage, the RV's probably totaled."

Cole decided to wait until eight to call Scott; he knew they wouldn't be back until later in the afternoon.

"Good morning, Cole. What's up?" Scott said.

"Well, partner, it's not such a good morning after all. This morning around 3:15 someone torched your RV and garage—"

"You've got to be shitting me!" I shouted into the phone.

"No, pal, I'm not. I wish I were. I was parked on your street about two houses down when I noticed the flames reflecting in your neighbors' windows. I couldn't see anyone around, but the garage was on fire. I called 911 and the fire department came right away. The garage can be saved, but—"

"Oh, God!" I moaned.

"The RV's totaled, but the garage can be repaired."

I muttered something obscene.

"For the last two nights I've been watching your place. There'd been nothing out of the ordinary. I didn't fall asleep, partner, I promise. After the firemen left I checked around where a side window had been broken out, but there weren't any footprints directly under the window the person used to gain entrance. I'll guess the gas can won't have any prints on it either. I'll have it checked anyway."

"I'm at the fuel dock now. As soon as we're done here, we're heading home. We should arrive back around three this afternoon."

15

Is there something wrong?" Kory was asking me.

I relayed the bad news, and we headed straight for home. As soon as we were past the marker buoys, I pushed the throttle forward.

"How long will it take us to get to Marinette?" Kory asked.

I was so absorbed in my thoughts that her question did not register.

"Scott?" she said again.

"Oh, I'm sorry. What did you say?"

"I asked, 'How long will it take us to get back home?'"

"I think it may be five to six hours, if we don't encounter any problems," I said.

"I'm going below and work on my book. Let me know if you need anything," She slipped out of sight.

The water was a little choppy, but I had the throttle at nearly full speed and was keeping watch for other craft. I was hoping Kory could still be able to use her laptop and get some work done on her novel. The ride wasn't terribly smooth, but I wasn't slowing down for anything I didn't have to.

Two hours later I noticed that the engine temperature was rising. I cut back to half-speed. After a few minutes it started cooling down and dropped into a normal range. We weren't hugging the shoreline any longer; in fact, we couldn't see land to any side. The last thing I wanted was to break down way out here in the deepest part of the lake and away from the major waterways.

Kory came up from below deck. "Is everything all right?"

"Yeah," I said, "We're fine." But I didn't feel reassured one bit.

"The yacht may be, but I can tell by your voice that you're not," she said. "I'll fix you a drink. Maybe it will calm your nerves."

"It's a little early," I replied.

"It may be, but I think it will help." She disappeared below deck again.

I couldn't believe how much my easy-going, slow-paced life had changed lately.

Kory came up holding two glasses filled with ice and a bottle of Scotch and some soda. She poured one for both of us. "This should take the edge off."

I continued the rest of the journey at a little under 30 knots without overheating the engine, which added another hour to our arrival time. After Kory and I secured the yacht, we headed directly to my place. Cole was waiting for us.

"Anything new?" I asked.

"Not really. The fire inspector is out back going over everything," Cole said.

"Let's join him," I said.

Tom Strughold, whom I knew from the Marinette Fire Department, looked up from the pile of scorched debris that surrounded my blackened RV. "Hello, Mr. St. Germain," he said.

"Hello, Tom. Have you found anything yet?"

"Well, only that the accelerant used was gasoline. And it was started in the inside rear of the RV. However, it had nothing to do with the RV's gas tank or engine. It appears to have been set intentionally from an outside source."

"So...," I said, "it was clearly arson."

"Sure seems that way," Strughold said.

Oh, God. One damn thing after another! I'd need to call the insurance company and get started on the claim process. They'd have to complete their job before I could have the RV removed and start repairs on the building. After that, I'd arrange to have the RV hauled away. *Damn, what's next?*

"Sorry about all this, Kory." I turned to her. "I'll take you home now."

"Thanks, hon." She gazed up at me, looking nearly as worried as I felt. "I want to check on Papa as soon as possible. Then I'll snuggle up to my computer and work a bit more on the book."

I wasn't pissed at Cole; he had done what he could. The person who did this had figured out how he could get away with it without being seen. None of the neighbors had seen anything suspicious or heard anyone breaking into the garage. If there were any footprints by the broken window, they had been trampled by the firemen in their attempt to put out the fire.

"Hey, Cole? What's going on with your Candy?" I had a good friend here with me who had his own set of problems.

"We cut her boyfriend lose after he paid his outstanding warrants," Cole said. "He and my ex checked out of the motel and headed back home. The Madison PD will be waiting for him—I made sure of that. It'd be my guess that she's not in the market for a new home just now." He stood there beside me, hands shoved deep in his pockets, still staring at the charred remains in my garage. "Some good news, though. I've met a new lady. Very nice. She works at the local hospital. She's a new doctor who's serving her third year residency there. A real looker too. Her name's Beth. Maybe the four of us could get together for dinner some evening soon."

"Sounds like a good idea," I answered, but my heart wasn't in anything just now.

16

Back at the motel, Manny Bruso's burner phone was buzzing. "Yeah?" he answered.

"Have you done anything else to our mark?"

"Yeah. I burnt up his garage and torched his RV."

"Good. He's probably going out of his mind trying to figure out who's behind his problems."

"Hey, Mo. I need a different car. Folks around here have seen this one a few times now and may have the license number."

"I understand. I'll send you another one the same way we did last time. I'll get rid of the Mustang. Manny, lay low until I call you."

"Okay, have your guy bring more cash at the same

time," Manny said. "This motel living is for shit." He clicked off. He needed to find a woman to spend time with. He hadn't been laid in over a month. And he also needed to find another motel right away.

Manny packed up his bags and strolled down to the manager's office, trying his best to avoid the blinking red light in the upper corner of the office over the desk. Surveillance cameras made him nervous. He hopped in the car and left in search of new digs. He located another motel in Marinette, but didn't check in. Instead, he parked the Mustang at the bus station parking lot and called a cab to take him back. He didn't want the manager wondering about him checking in with a black car when a different car would shortly be parked in front.

The car and cash were delivered two days later. Manny's new ride was a deep red 2013 Chevy Camaro with Illinois plates. He had taken a cab back to the bus station and met Mo's guy for the exchange. He drove back to the motel and checked into Room 109, first floor on the end. It didn't take much getting settled. He flipped on the TV; in the movie that was playing a couple was making love. He vowed that tonight he'd find a woman to have sex with, by force if necessary.

On the eastern edge of town was a community known as Minikani, where the old fur traders had set up shop back in the 1800s. That area also boasted quite a few taverns and bars, and Manny began his search for a sex partner at a popular place called The Oar House.

It was nine o'clock on Friday night, and the bar was in full swing. Manny took a seat near the back door where he could observe everyone coming and going. Most of the customers were probably couples that lived near by.

"What would you like to drink?" a pretty waitress asked him. She had long shimmering red hair and twinkling blue eyes.

"A beer," Manny said

"Draft or bottle?"

"A bottle."

"What kind?"

"Bud."

"Need a glass, mister?"

"For Christ's sake!" Manny exploded angrily. "Just bring me a bottle of Bud!"

"Sorry," the cute waitress said, looking hurt. She was back quickly with Manny's order.

"I'm sorry I barked at you." Manny placed a one hundred dollar bill on the table. "Keep the change." He smiled at her and she smiled back.

"What's your name?" Manny asked.

"It's Amber. And what's yours, if I may ask?"

"Just call me Sam."

"Thanks for the great tip." She winked as she walked away from the table.

"That's just for *you,* cutie," he warned. "Don't go sharing now." She'd better know not to go spreading word of his generosity.

As the evening wore on, Manny aka "Sam" switched to hammering down boilermakers, leaving a large tip each time. At one in the morning, most of the patrons had left.

"Hey, Amber!" He waved and she came over to his booth. "How about we go out for breakfast?"

"Okay, Sam. That'd be nice. I get off in thirty minutes."

"I'll wait for you in the parking lot," he said as he pushed open the door and left the tavern.

The parking lot was dimly lit. Manny had preferred to leave his new ride hidden as much as possible in the shadows. He had not talked with anyone while he was in the bar, and no one but Amber had visited his table. Fairly certain he had gone unnoticed, he wasn't planning to take her to any breakfast either. His plans involved a bit more violence—he liked violence. When Amber finally came out, he planned to overpower her and knock her unconscious. Then he would put her in the passenger seat and drive deep into the nearby woods. He'd rape her first and then kill her.

Standing in the shadows, Manny waited until Amber stepped from the tavern, but she wasn't alone. A tall, hefty man was walking her to her car. There were only five cars still in the parking lot, not counting Manny's Camaro. The big guy turned around and went back inside.

Amber was sitting in her car and seemed to be on her cell phone, apparently talking to someone. She spotted Sam leaning against his car. She left her car and walked over to him, tucking the phone in her pocket.

"I just talked to my sister and told her to meet us at the Gateway Cafe," she said. "It's the only place open this time in the morning."

"How old's your sister"

"Twenty-eight—same as me. We're identical twins."

"She's not married—or bringing along a boyfriend?"

"No." Amber laughed. "You'll be getting two for one."

"Getting what?" Sam asked.

"Just kidding," she said, her tone light and teasing.

"Hop in," Sam said.

Amber was laughing again. "No. I'll take my car and you can follow me."

Two for one and twins—this could get interesting, he thought.

Manny followed Amber to the Gateway Cafe and parked beside her. There were only a few customers inside, one of whom was Amber's sister.

"Sam this is my sister, Alicia," Amber said. "Alicia, this is Sam." They shook hands and sat down in the booth.

To Manny, it seemed almost like Amber was looking in a mirror. She and Alicia had the same smile and mannerisms. They even combed their hair the same. A waitress brought menus and coffee. The girls were busy chatting with each other, while Manny was looking around for cameras or for other people who might be watching them.

The waitress returned to take their order. The sisters ordered the same hearty breakfast, but Sam wanted only toast and coffee. Amber and Alicia were doing most of the talking and about matters he had no interest in.

"Sam, are you new to this area?" Amber asked.

"Yeah, I am. I just took a part-time job here. I'll probably go back to Chicago in a month."

"What do you do?" Alicia asked.

"Well...." Sam hesitated. "I'm a private investigator."

"Oh! That sounds exciting," Amber said.

The sisters even sounded alike.

"Tell us about it."

"Afraid I can't talk about it," Sam said.

"So you work for the government?"

"Can't say." Sam smiled his best smile for the two pretty women.

"Well, let's talk about something else," Amber said. "Thank you for all the tips you gave me tonight." She turned and whispered in Alicia's ear.

"You're very welcome, sweetie."

"You're very generous. I was wondering if you might be interested in some additional recreation with me and my sister, like dessert after breakfast." Amber's voice was low, sexy, and suggestive.

"Do you still have the energy after working all night?" Sam asked.

Amber and Alicia exchanged a glance. They nodded and laughed.

"What's this little adventure going to cost?" Sam said, still forcing a smile. They were messing with his plans, but he'd always fantasized about doing twins. Didn't most guys?

"Three hundred. You'll really like what you get for your money," Alicia said.

"I take it you two've done this before."

"Oh… once in a while," Amber answered vaguely.

"Where?" Sam asked.

"My place," Amber answered.

"Any kids or dogs around?"

"Nope." Amber was laughing again. "It'll be just the three of us."

"Let's go for it." Manny paid the bill, leaving only an average tip this time.

Earlier Amber had been thinking she'd keep Sam all to herself. He'd be a real meal ticket. *Those tips!* Then she thought of her sister. Together they could rob him of his cash.

If he went to the police, they could say that he attacked them and tried to rape them. With two against one—especially two pretty, auburn-haired young twins—they figured the police would believe them, not some ratty-looking G-man. They had done it twice before. Both men were from out of town and married, so they had kept their months shut.

"This guy may be different. If he really is who he says he is, he may be tight with the cops," Amber said to her sister as they were driving home.

"Maybe we should just do him for the three hundred and call it good," Alicia suggested.

Manny was following them through the twisting streets of Minikani. They seemed to be the only traffic out early in the morning.

Amber giggled. "I bet he has no idea where the hell he is."

"Yes," Alicia said. "All the old homes on our street look alike."

"I wouldn't worry. It's a small town and he can find his way back easy enough. Especially if he's really a government agent." The sisters were laughing as they parked in the driveway.

"You can park on the street!" Alicia called out to him.

Inside, the girls led Sam to their master bedroom. They started slowly removing his clothes. One would take off his belt, the other pulled off his shirt. They alternated, each lavishing him with tongue-deep kisses. Sometimes Alicia would tease him, flicking her tongue at his nipples. Amber let her hand lightly touch his penis.

"You're not really ready, are you?" Amber teased him, stroking his erection that was more than ready. Sam lay naked on the bed, immediately rock hard and quivering.

"Have you ever had two girls at the same time before?" Alicia asked.

"Yeah, a couple of times—but never twins."

"Well, this will be very special." Amber was cooing into his ear. "For an added fee, we'll do each other for your enjoyment."

"How much more?"

"A hundred each," Amber said.

"Deal! But I want to participate while it's happening," Sam said.

The girls excused themselves and went into the bathroom together. "We'll be right back."

"I don't think we should rob him yet, because he's

obviously well heeled. I think we can milk this deal a few more times before we take him for everything," Amber whispered to her sister.

"I'm in," Alicia agreed.

They came back to Sam, already lying naked on the bed, and their threesome was underway.

Manny had needed to think quickly and figure out what he ought to do. Should it be sex—wild and crazy sex—or a double murder? However, it had been every bit as good as the twins had promised: they had bought the right to live a little longer.

It was after five thirty when Manny arrived back at the motel. He sank down on his bed, smiling and recalling the previous two hours. He leaned back and fell asleep.

17

Scott's phone buzzed. He picked up; the display showed it was Cole. "Hey, bud. How you're doing?"

"Beth has the weekend off for a change. Would you and Kory would like to join us for dinner?"

"It's fine with me. I'll check with her and call you right back."

I dialed her phone, the number fixed in my memory. "Good morning, darling," I said when she answered.

"You sound in a better mood than when I saw you last."

"I am. The insurance company says that I'm one hundred percent covered, but I'm not calling about that. Cole's asked us to join him and his new lady friend for dinner on Sunday. Is it okay with you?"

"Sure. I'd like to meet her. Did he say where we'll be going?"

"No, but I'll get the details later. How is your granddad doing?"

"He's trying to adjust to having a roommate. He says the guy snores so loud he can't hear his TV." Kory laughed. "That's where I am right now. I'm going to wheel him down to the little lake they have here. He wants to go fishing."

"You two have fun. I'll call back later."

"Okay. Love you," she said and clicked off.

Did I hear right? Did she really say "love you?" It was Saturday, and Simone was off on the weekend. I needed to catch up on some work, actually more than I'd expected. I'd been in my office about an hour when the phone rang. "Scott St. Germain," I answered automatically.

"Hi, boss. It's Digger. We've been busy the past few days. This guy Mike O'Bannon—or 'Mo' as everyone calls him—is quite the heavy hitter. I've been working with my friend, the PI. We found out that Claude Curry had borrowed money from Mo to keep his company afloat. Poor Claude was having a rough time paying it back." Digger paused a moment, and I heard him turning the pages of the little notebook he always kept handy. "We think that's why Mo came up to visit Mr. Curry and was in town for the poker game."

"Wow! That's news to me. I was Claude's attorney—and I never knew that," I said. "I had thought Claude told me everything about his business. Maybe that's tied into Claude's murder some way."

"We've found out a lot about this guy—drug trafficking, prostitution, stolen cars, and chop shops. If you can ever get him into court, he'll be in quicksand," Digger said.

"You guys did a great job, Digger." I really needed him back in town. "Figure out what I owe your friend, write up your report, come home, and give me your bill."

"See you, Monday, boss," Digger said and the phone went silent.

I'd barely hung up when the phone rang again.

"Hello. Mr. St. Germain? This is Ken Bentley."

I scratched my head. "Yes?" *Who?*

"You and your lady friend were going to have dinner at my place the other night. The Coyote Moon, remember? My yacht is tied up along side yours at the marina."

"Oh, yes, Mr. Bentley." It was coming back to me—the terrible night with my smashed windshield. Too much had been happening of late. "I remember now. I believe you wanted to talk to me."

"Yes, that's why I was calling. Several nights back—I'm not sure now exactly when it was—I was staying overnight on my boat. I got up to take a leak and then walked out on deck. There was a man hoisting himself out of the water and up onto our dock. I'd swear he was wearing only underpants. And he was carrying a kind of tote bag over his shoulder."

"Did you get a good look at him, Mr. Bentley?"

"No. I'm sorry. It was after dark, and the only light was from the moon. I sort of thought it might be you. But a few minutes later, he got back in the water and swam away. I didn't know what to think, and I didn't report it to anyone. Then later I heard the DEA had come aboard the *Snow Flake* a day or so later. So I thought you should know."

"Thanks, Mr. Bentley," I said. "That helps clear up several things that have taken place lately."

18

Manny gazed out the window of the motel, noticing there was no one at the swimming pool. It was noon on a clear, sunny day. He needed to get out of the room for awhile. Taking off his shirt and stretching out in one of the lounge chairs to get some rays seemed like a grand idea.

Shirtless and barefoot, Manny walked to the pool entrance and found a padded chaise lounge near the shallow end. He slipped on his sunglasses, laid back, and soon fell asleep. Half an hour later a family with three young children came out to the pool and sat down next to him. The three kids, ranging between eight and twelve, started running, yelling, and jumping into the pool, splashing water on him.

Startled, Manny awoke. "What the fuck is going on?" he yelled. Noticing the children's mother sitting beside him, he turned to her. "You'd better take care of those little shits or I'll drown 'em."

The mother drew back, shocked. "They're just kids. You don't need to talk like that to them or us!"

The children's father leaped from his chair and started toward Manny. His wife reached out and grabbed her husband's arm, restraining him. "Honey, please sit down."

Still visibly upset, the children's father continued talking to Manny. "You have no business talking like that! Who do you think you are anyway?"

Manny responded, "Fuck you!"

The family gathered up their towels and sun tan lotion and left the pool area, headed for the manager's office.

Soon the manager was standing beside his lounge chair, staring down at him in disapproval. "Mr. Smith, this pool is for the enjoyment of all our clients. You're not to use foul language around any of our guests. Is that understood?"

Manny didn't want to draw any more attention. "Yes, you're right. I lost my temper and I'm sorry."

"Thank you, Mr. Smith." The manager returned to his office. Manny thought he looked as smug as though he had just won a high school debate.

Manny went back to his room, brooding.

He wasn't sorry at all. If anything he was thinking about how he could get back at those people for squealing on him. His temper had gotten him in trouble almost all his life, and he'd never found a way to control it. Nowadays he didn't even try. He'd come to take pleasure in intimidating people and controlling them.

Manny had left school in the tenth grade; he had never developed more than the intellectual and emotional development of an eighth grader. He'd never married, and his life of crime started when he was very young. Now he worked as a hit man; he had nine murders to his credit. He wore them like a badge of honor; he was a loner with a mean and angry streak. However, he was paid handsomely for his services.

He spent his winters in Florida, roaming the beaches and looking for women to victimize, and he had been fairly successful at it. He would leave the Sunshine State when Mr. O'Bannon had a job for him to take care of, then he return to Florida. During the summer months, Manny lived in Cicero, near Chicago. His parents had died when he was young, and he didn't have any brothers or sisters. He became a ward of the state at an early age, in and out of foster homes most of his younger life. Soon the streets had become his home.

19

It was Friday morning. I was busy at my desk poring over a business contract for one of my clients.

The phone rang and Simone answered. "Yes, he's in. May I put you on hold for a moment? Thank you." She pushed the hold button. "Boss, there's a man on the line who says he has a picture of someone leaving Claude Curry's garage the morning of the murder."

I looked up, amazed. I could hardly believe my ears. "Did the caller tell you his name?"

"No, boss. He just asked for you."

I grabbed for the desk phone. "Hello. Scott St. Germain here. May I ask who's calling?"

"My name is Roger Gibbons," the caller began. "I live directly behind the Currys' home. I'm an amateur stargazer, you see. Before sunrise the day of the murder I was on my back deck looking at the sky through my telescope."

And just what did stargazing have to do with murder? I wondered but let the man continue. "Yes, Mr. Gibbons?"

"Well, out of the corner of my eye, I noticed movement down on the ground. I swung the scope around to see if I could tell what it was and focused on the object." Gibbons paused. "It was a man crouched over and running away from the Currys' garage. I have a camera attached to the telescope to take pictures of certain stars. So I snapped a quick shot of the man."

"Why haven't you called the police?" I was glad to have some potential new evidence, but I was also mighty exasperated with this caller. Was he just another crackpot?

"Well, my wife and I were leaving on our vacation early that morning. We returned yesterday. We just learned from our neighbor that poor Mr. Curry had been killed," Gibbons said. "So, then I downloaded all my pictures from the camera and there it was. There's a person dressed in dark clothing who appears to be carrying a knife. From the angle you can't see the man's face. He had on gloves and a cap. I called you because I heard you were the Currys' attorney."

"I'll have Detective Cole Dominic from the Marinette PD pick up the photo. Thank you for calling," I said and hung up. I called Cole immediately and passed the story on to him.

"I'll make a copy of the photo for our department and one for you too," Cole told me. "The original goes to the Wisconsin State Police," he added.

"By the way, I've been meaning to ask you," I said before he could hang up. "How did you and your new lady friend meet?"

"I went to a medical training seminar, and Beth was the guest speaker. We chatted a bit afterwards. I asked her out for dinner. She accepted and that was that," Cole said.

"I'll make reservations for the four us at The Crew's Quarter's," I said. "How's Saturday at seven?"

"Great," Cole said. "That's a day off for Beth."

After he hung up, I started thinking about what Bentley had told me. Whoever he had seen must have been the person who planted the cocaine. He also was familiar with the layout of the yacht. It certainly couldn't be Mo. There was no way he could hoist himself out of the water and up onto the dock. He was too damn heavy for that. He must have sent someone with instructions on where to hide the package.

Digger called, interrupting my deep thinking as I tried to sort through all the odd happenings of the past month. He wanted to know whether he could come over to my place to hand in his report. He's probably more interested in getting paid than giving me his report. I had no problem with that, because he had put in the time and effort. "Sure, Digger," I told him. "I'll be here all day." I hung up and returned to the puzzle of coincidences—or were they?

First Claude was murdered. If the person who killed him was a local, why did it happen? There wasn't any evidence of robbery around Claude's body or in the home. Mrs. Curry said she wasn't aware of anyone who had a grudge against Claude.

My conclusion was that it couldn't be someone from around here. If the murderer was from out of town, he must be staying at a motel or at a bed and breakfast. Maybe I should check the motels in Menominee first. It was a long shot, but I needed to get to the bottom of this. Unfortunately, all I had to go on was a not very clear picture of a guy leaving Claude's garage.

Digger showed up about noon. We took care of business and had a nice conversation. I got around to telling him what I had planned concerning Claude's murder.

"I think that's a good idea," he said. "I'd like to go with you."

I faced him directly, meeting his gaze. "The meter's not running on this one."

"That's okay with me." Digger shrugged. "I've got nothing planned for today anyway."

There were plenty of motels in the Menominee area. We decided to map them by location to cut down on driving time. We identified twenty-two, although a few were outside the city limits but were close enough that they should be considered.

"I'll drive. You can navigate," I said.

"Let's start from the farthest away and work into the city. The Dockside Inn will be our first stop. It's 28445 Waters' Edge Drive. That's off M35, two miles past the city limits," Digger announced. Each time we stopped at a motel, we would ask for the owner or the manager. Our questions were always the same: "Have you noticed any suspicious person from out of state who is staying for an extended time?" Then we would show the picture of the mysterious man. Each gave us the same answer: "Most of our guests are from outside of the area." *and* "No, we haven't had anyone like that staying with us."

We had covered fourteen motels and were now inside the city. Our next stop was the Dodge Motel on Rio Vista Drive. It was on the opposite side of the Menominee River and directly across from my house in Marinette.

"Hello, my name is Scott St. Germain. My friend and I were hoping you might be able to help us."

"What is it you need?"

"Have you had or still have a guest from out of state that seemed out of the ordinary—"

"Well," the manager interrupted me. "As a matter of fact, there was one fella' that stayed in his room for several weeks and had food delivered to him. He never gave me any trouble though."

I showed the manager the picture.

"It's hard to say if that's him or not."

"What name did he register under?" I asked.

"Sam Smith," the manager said.

"Is he still here?"

The manager shook his head. "Sorry. He checked out several days ago."

"Can you describe him?" I asked.

"Well.... Let's see. He was about six foot. Less than two hundred pounds, I'd guess. Has bad teeth and a big scar on the left side of his face. Receding hair, although he's probably about mid-forties." The manager paused a moment. "You know the reason I remember him so well? He arrived in a cab. Then a couple days later he said he'd bought a car. It had Illinois plates. I wondered where he could have found a car like that around here."

"Do you have the license number of the car he was driving?"

"Yes, I think I do. Let me check my files."

The manager worked his computer. As he read the file, he started reading the information to us slowly.

"Here it is. It's a black Ford Mustang. Illinois plate Q7W4843."

"Did this guy Sam say where he was headed?"

"No. He just paid his bill in cash one day and left."

"I'll be damned. Kory was right. That's the car she's seen that's been harassing us.

"I'll call my friend in Chicago and get the name of the registered owner." Digger pulled out his cell phone and punched in a number. "Hey, bro. I've got an Illinois plate I'd like you to run ASAP. It's Q7W4843. Give me a shout as soon as you get something."

"Thanks for your help," I told the manager. We left his office and climbed into my Jeep. As we were starting back toward my place, Digger's phone buzzed.

"Yeah?" he answered it quickly. He kept nodding his head as he listened to the person on the other end of the line. "No shit." As he hung up his smile turned to a frown.

"What gives?" I asked.

"The plate is from a stolen car, originally issued to a white Toyota Avalon. The Avalon owner reported the vehicle went missing three months ago. It probably ended up in a chop shop, and the plate was switched to another vehicle," Digger said.

"Yeah, to a certain black Ford Mustang." I said. How discouraging to be so close and then to be messed up like this.

"I'll bet he's still in the area. We'll have to start over

with all the motels, now that we have the car and plate information," Digger said.

It was after one and I was famished. "We need to discuss this thoroughly. And I need lunch."

20

Dorothy Marie's Pie Shop is two block away. I go there all the time. Best pies in the Twin Cities as far as I'm concerned," Digger said.

"Let's go," I said. "But I'll need a real lunch, more than pie."

We spread the map out on the café's table, trying to decide whether we should call with the new information or go back to each of the motels we had already covered. We finally agreed to call them.

I took half the list and Digger took the others. One by one, we called each of them, but none had anything to add.

"We still have the rest of our list to contact," I said.

"Yeah, I can give it another hour," Digger said.

We finished lunch and stopped at four more motels, with no results. Soon the hour was up, and Digger had to leave. There were four places left, so I called on them myself, still with no results. Then it came to me. What about any motels in the Marinette area? The wind had suddenly picked up and dark clouds were coming in from the west. It looked like rain any minute.

The Marinette idea would have to wait for another day. I needed to get back and discuss several urgent business matters with Simone. I also wanted to call Kory to let her know what we had learned about the black Ford Mustang.

Last, I called Cole and told him what Digger and I had learned, especially the information about the Ford Mustang.

"Whoa, Scott!" Cole interrupted Scott. "The description you got at the Dodge Inn is the exact same one Punky gave us about the guy who hired him to spray-paint your yacht."

"I'll be damned, it is! Why I hadn't noticed it before?"

"Let's get hold of Punky and see if he's seen Sam around lately," Cole said.

"Do you have a phone number or address for him?"

"I'm sure it's in his file. He's been here a number of times in the past. However, if we don't, we can always call Menominee PD," Cole said.

"Are we still on for tomorrow evening?" Scott asked.

"Sure thing," Cole said. "We're looking forward to it."

"I hope the weather clears up."

"Me too. If it does, maybe the four of us could take a nice romantic walk on the beach after dinner."

"Hey, bro," Scott said. "You're really getting into the romance thing."

"Gotta do something, you know. I don't have a yacht to impress her with." Cole chuckled.

"If you need it, you know it's available to you," Scott said. "Maybe the four of us could take an overnight cruise."

"Sounds great. The printer's spitting out Punky's file. I'll call you back, Scott," Cole said as he clicked off. Within minutes, he was dialing Punky's cell phone. "Punky, Cole Dominic here."

"Officer Dominic, how ya' doin'?" He sounded like he had been drinking or was high on something.

"I'm fine, Punky. Do you remember when you told me about this guy Sam that you met a short while ago?"

"Yeah."

"Have you seen him around since we talked last?"

"Nope, just that once," Punky said.

"Well, if you do, give me a call. Remember, it could help you out in the future," Cole said and hung up.

Cole redialed Scott's number. "No luck with Punky, but I think he'll contact me if he sees his buddy Sam."

~

By Saturday morning, the storm had passed, and the weather forecast was for bright and sunny skies and temperatures in the high-seventies for the next five days.

I called Kory to remind her about our date with Cole and Beth in the evening.

"I have it on my schedule. Do you need to make reservations?" she asked.

"I've already taken care of it," I said.

"The landscapers are here now. They're taking care of Papa's property," Kory said. "It always looks so nice when they finish."

"I'm doing the same thing to mine in a little while. It probably won't look as good as a professional job."

"Your place always looks beautiful, but you should hire someone to take care of it. It would help free your time, you know," Kory said. "You have people take care your yacht don't you?"

"Yes, but that's different," I said.

"Let's change the subject. How do you want me to dress for tonight?"

"Sweetheart, you're in charge of that. You always look so stunning," I told her and I was being totally honest.

She laughed. "Good answer!"

"Could you stay overnight?" I asked.

"I was hoping you'd ask me. It's been several days since we've been together, and I'm missing you."

I could hear the longing in her voice. She was right: she had a way of making all of me react. I had missed her too.

Kory and I had arrived a few minutes early and were seated at my favorite table overlooking the river. By the time Cole and Beth arrived we had already placed our drink order but hadn't received it yet. I grinned and slapped Cole lightly on the back; Beth was a striking woman.

After introductions all around, we all sat down again. The ladies were seated together and seemed to hit it off right away.

Beth leaned forward. "This is the first time I've been here. It's a beautiful place."

"They have a great menu too," Cole said. "The food is always wonderful."

Conversation flowed easily between us. Beth was

describing her entrance into the field of medicine.

"But how did you come to Marinette?" Kory asked.

Our meals arrived and soon the wine was flowing. Beth never had a chance to answer. Further chatter seemed unnecessary; the food at the Crew's Quarters is that superb.

"The evening's still young," Cole said when we had finished. "Would you lovely ladies like to take a moonlight walk on the beach?"

We agreed and left the restaurant, strolling along a brick path that led down to the sandy beach.

"Scott?" Beth said. "I hear that you have a yacht."

"Yes, that's true." I wondered what else Cole had told her.

"Do you use it often?"

"He's taken me on two trips last month," Kory said. "We had a wonderful time."

I was suddenly having a flash of inspiration. "Would you like to take an overnight trip to Sheboygan? That's where Kory lives. She can show us around while we're there."

"I'd love that," Kory said.

"Well, what do you two think?" I turned back to Cole and Beth.

"I'm game. How about you, Beth?" Cole asked.

"Sounds great!" Beth sounded excited. "I'll need to make arrangements at the hospital. Getting two days off in a row is a challenge."

"If Beth can get off, let's plan on leaving next Friday," I said.

"You know that will leave your house unguarded." Cole was recalling the RV incident.

"Yeah. I'll ask Simone to stay the weekend. She'll take care of K9 too. Then Digger can watch the outside."

"That should work," Cole said.

21

Amber had given Manny her cell number the last time they were together. Shouldn't he be getting some stirrings again? What man wouldn't recall the exciting threesome he had had with them?

"We were wondering when you'd call," Amber said when she answered, her voice low and alluring.

"Do you girls have any plans for tonight?" he asked her.

"No, I lost my job at the tavern. We could use the extra money right about now. Is my place okay?" she asked "Can you find it again?"

"Yeah, it's in my GPS. What time should I get there?"

"Honey," she purred. "You can come as early as you want—and as often as we can make you." She was pleased with the little pun, but Manny the G-man probably didn't get it.

"Is eight o'clock okay?" Manny said.

"Works for us," she responded. This time he was really going to pay.

"You girls think of something new to add to our get together. That will get me real excited."

"That's not a problem, sugar. You just bring lots of money." Amber was laughing as she clicked off.

~

Manny was wondering what he should do about the sisters. Should they live or die of unnatural causes? The more he thought about it, the more he decided against it. He needed to concentrate on what he was getting paid for.

The girls could wait, although he actually enjoyed killing people. Usually he would go to where ever the mark was and do the job quickly—like with Claude Curry. Just in and out. This time it was different. Mo wanted the attorney to suffer. Manny felt that he was spending far too long in one place and that could only lead to mistakes.

Even in a hick town like this, with cops stepping on their own dicks, they would eventually figure things out. He'd play it safe and let the girls live—at least for now. After he popped the attorney and his girlfriend, then he could do the sisters. He must tie up all the loose ends.

22

On Friday afternoon Kory and I greeted Cole and Beth on the dock beside the *Snow Flake*. Soon they'd brought their gear aboard, and I spent about twenty minutes showing Cole and Beth around.

After everyone was settled in, we headed for Lake Michigan and then south to Sheboygan. There was a slow roll to the water, but the boat cut through it as smoothly as a knife through butter—another beautiful day on the water.

"Should we sleep aboard tonight?" Kory asked me. "Or would you like to stay at my place?"

"I'm not sure." This might be awkward. "You see, I don't know if they've had the pleasure of sleeping together yet or not. I'll have to ask Cole."

Kory grinned and looked out at the water. Cole and Beth were holding hands, sitting on the top deck enjoying the cruise.

"Hey Cole!" I called up to him. "Pop us a couple of beers. They're in the galley fridge. I'm stuck driving this old tub."

Everyone laughed.

"I'm on it," Cole replied and clambered down the ladder from the top deck.

When he handed me the beer, I asked. "Hey, Cole. Are you and—" I nodded toward the upper deck. "Normally it wouldn't be any of my business, but I need to know about sleeping arrangements tonight. Are you two bunk mates yet?"

He burst out laughing. "Almost."

"What do you mean, 'almost'?"

"Well, we had enjoyed a romantic evening, dining, dancing, and such. Then we went to her place. We were naked and getting into bed, when my beeper went off. I was on call and had to leave.... So 'almost,'" he said again. We clinked bottles and laughed.

"So bunking together tonight wouldn't be a problem?" I said.

"Not a problem at all," he answered. "I've turned off my beeper too!"

Kory was making a plate of snacks while we each sipped on another beer. She continued talking with Beth. "Do you know what the Mile High Club is?"

"Oh, I sure do." She giggled. "I once dated a guy who owned an airplane."

"Well, Scott and I have formed a new club called the Mile Out Club. So far we're the only members."

"How does it work?" Beth asked.

"Same rules, just a mile out instead of up," Kory said.

Beth winked at Cole. "Maybe we'll become the next new members."

"Are you girls having fun?" I asked.

"You bet," Kory said.

"We're approaching the Sturgeon Bay Canal in Door County. We'll use it to cut though to Lake Michigan, then south to Sheboygan," I said.

We were cruising slower while in the canal, admiring the beautiful homes and farms on both sides. When we reached Lake Michigan the water was a bit rougher but no one seemed to mind.

I found an FM station on the radio in the main salon. There was some great music, and I turned it up so everyone could hear. The ladies changed into swimwear and stretched out on the top deck. Cole and I started discussing what we could do to unravel the strange events of the past few weeks.

"This has gone on far too long," I said. "We don't have anything concrete, just supposition."

"Yeah, I know. But we do know that Mo is involved in cocaine. It was discovered on board the yacht, and it wasn't yours."

"You're right. Could it have been left there by accident?"

"Bullshit!" Cole muttered. "What do you think that guy was doing aboard in the middle of the night a couple weeks ago? I think Mo sent him up here to set you up."

"Even if you're right, Cole, Mo probably has an airtight alibi."

"We have to find the guy that's still here doing this shit."

"I checked all the motels. I got a lead on the Ford Mustang and a description of the guy, but now that even seems like a dead end."

Cole's cell phone buzzed. "You're not going to believe this—it's Punky! Hey, Punky," Cole answered. "What do ya' need?"

"I just saw that guy Sam. Ya' know, the one I told you about before. Well, he's driving a bright red Chevy Camaro. I was hangin' with a buddy at his gas station. Sam pulled in and was pumpin' his gas."

"Did you get his plate number?" Cole asked.

"Shit, no! I didn't want him to see me—he scares me. I did see the plate was from Illinois though."

"I'm in the middle of Lake Michigan on a fishing trip. I'll be back in town Monday. I want you to come in and talk with me. You're not in any trouble. In fact, you've just earned a few brownie points," Cole said and clicked off.

"We should arrive in time for dinner ashore. Is there any place special you'd like to go?"

"Oh, yes!" Kory exclaimed. "My all time favorite is Lino Ristorante Italiano, and it's close to the marina on Pier Drive. The best Italian food I've ever experienced," Kory said. "It's a casual and romantic place."

"Then that's where we'll go. Should we call for reservations?" I asked.

"Most definitely. It's Friday evening," Kory said. She already had the number in her cell phone. A couple minutes later our reservations were set for seven.

"Now, sweetie, how should we handle the sleeping arrangements tonight?" I asked.

"I think you and I should stay at my place. We'll let Cole and Beth have the master cabin here on the yacht. It would be more romantic for them." She smiled her infectious smile.

We located the marina and pulled into a vacant slip. As usual, Kory handled her first mate duties and helped tie up. Everyone had changed into casual attire, ready for dinner.

I searched for the marina office but it was closed. I'd pay them in the morning.

"Let's get a cab." Kory was looking in her phone for taxi service. "The restaurant is about a mile away." The courteous cab driver delivered us fifteen minutes early. "Perfect timing! We're in for a special treat, I promise. The food, the service, and the wine list are the best one could ever hope for." She sounded like the voice of experience.

Afterwards, everyone agreed that it was truly an excellent dinner. At eight, I called a car rental agency. After giving them all the necessary information, I asked them to deliver the vehicle to the marina parking area in about an hour. Kory and Beth decided they wanted to walk, even though it was a mile back to the marina, enjoying the fresh cool air of evening. When they arrived, the rental car was waiting.

"Cole, you and Beth can enjoy the master cabin on the yacht and have a romantic evening. Kory and I will be at her place. We'll pick you up tomorrow morning at nine for breakfast and after that Kory can show us her town."

"Fine with us." Cole took Beth's hand and they walked toward the *Snow Flake.*

23

Kory's home was on the east side of the city on a hill. The back patio faced Lake Michigan, and at night the city lights twinkled below. It was a modest home in a nice neighborhood. She unlocked the front door and switched on the lights. "Home sweet home."

Looking around everything seemed to be in order. She gave me a quick tour ending in her bedroom.

"Now, my handsome yacht captain, we will shower. Then I'll allow you to maneuver me through the waves on my waterbed." She kissed me, slowly undressing me.

Later, we rode the rough seas until all was calm. Embracing at last, we were soon fast asleep in each others arms.

In the morning, Kory and I were exactly on time to pick up Cole and Beth, who were waiting where we'd left them last night. Kory recommended a place for breakfast, and we were on our way. Afterwards she directed us to other points of interest in the city and the day slipped away.

Sheboygan was settled in 1835 and currently had a population of approximately 50,000; for the most part, they enjoyed living in their quiet and beautiful city.

We slept aboard Saturday evening. After Kory and Beth fixed a tasty breakfast Sunday morning, we headed for home.

"Beth was telling me about your recently formed Mile Out Club," Cole said as we puttered out of the marina. "Can you tell me when we reach the point?"

"Sure thing, buddy." I winked. After twenty minutes, I signaled him with a thumbs-up.

Cole took Beth's hand and guided her below deck. A short while later, Cole stuck his head out. "Scott, I believe you have two new members," he announced. Beth followed him topside. She was blushing; Cole was smiling. "Meet the newest members of the Mile Out Club."

The day was bright and sunny, and the water was relatively calm. We made good time along the way. I projected we should arrive back home by late afternoon. Kory had been working on her book most of the way, while Beth stayed topside, stretched out on a beach towel. Cole and I were sharing a couple of beers and discussing the mystery man Sam.

Kory came up to join us. "I'm stuck," she said.

"What do you mean?" I asked.

"When we get to your place, I need you to help me on courtroom procedures."

"I'll be happy to," I said.

As we entered the mouth of the Menominee River, I slowed to a slow trawling speed, about 3 knots. The others started packing and tidying up the boat. After we docked, I took the trash bags to the marina dumpster.

Beth hugged Kory. "I've really enjoyed this."

"Yes," Kory said, "we should get together, just the two of us."

Cole kissed Beth goodbye, but they each needed to go their separate ways. Kory pulled out her phone; I knew she was calling her grandfather. They talked briefly, but Kory looked worried.

"Is everything okay?"

"I'm not sure. Papa's been running a low grade fever," she said.

"Do you want to drive over there first?" I asked.

"No, it's probably nothing to worry about. Let's just head to your place."

On our way home, I had a gnawing, gut feeling that something might be wrong at the house. To my surprise and relief, everything was in order.

Simone was there to greet us, holding K9 in her arms. "Hi, boss. How was your trip?"

"It worked out well. Everyone had a great time."

She set the tiny dog down on the floor. "I've been doing my homework and taking care of K9."

"Thanks for your help. There'll be extra in your check this week. I guess you know that, because you make out the checks for me to sign." We both laughed.

Simone gathered up what she'd brought with her for the weekend and waved goodbye to K9, who was whining and wagging his tiny tail as she left. "See you in the morning."

"Kory, would you like to spend the night?"

"I'll stay a short while, but then I'll have you run me home," she said. "I need to get back. I'd like to stay."

I wanted to delay her leaving; she was becoming a part of my life. "What was the courtroom information you needed?"

"Oh, yes. First, could you define an arraignment for me?"

"Well, an arraignment is the first part of a criminal procedure that occurs in a courtroom in front of a judge. The purpose is to provide the accused with a reading of the crime that he or she has been charged with. An arraignment must occur within seventy-two hours of the person's arrest or he may contend that his constitutional rights have been denied to a speedy trial."

Kory was taking notes, although she'd brought along a small recorder.

"Often arraignments are a multiple-step procedure," I continued. "The first part is having him—or her—appear in court, at which time he will be advised by the court of the right to be represented by an attorney or public defender. It also depends on whether it's a state or a federal charge or a felony or misdemeanor."

She nodded. "I understand."

"Then, once the accused is represented by counsel, he's expected to enter a plea. Parties can also waive the arraignment and enter a plea instead."

"Okay, got it." She stopped the recorder.

"Would you like something to drink?" I asked, still trying my best to keep her there with me.

"No thanks, Scott. Thanks for a wonderful weekend. But could you take me home now?" She hugged me, kissing me too, a long, warm kiss.

24

When Sam pulled up to Amber's house at eight in the evening, it was still light out. Kids were playing down the street on their bikes, riding over a homemade ramp. From somewhere in the distance, he heard music. Scenes like these reminded him of when he was a kid. It was one of the few good memories he could recall.

Amber answered the door. "Come in, Sam. How've you been?" She handed him a shot glass of whiskey.

"About the same," Sam said. He tipped back his head and downed the shot.

"We've missed you." Amber said. "We were wondering if you'd finished your business and left for Chicago."

"No, still working. Where's your sister?"

"Alicia stopped at the drug store. She's buying some special oils that you'll enjoy, but she's on her way."

Amber had rehearsed what they'd say to Sam. Alicia wasn't at a drug store but had gone to a friend's house to get the date rape drug Rohypnol, known on the street as a "roofie." They'd been planning carefully; this time they would take Sam for everything he had on him. At the agreed upon time, one of them would put the drug into his drink, while the other would keep him occupied and out of eyesight of the other. The drug might take up to an hour to take effect and they would need to keep him entertained for the entire time.

Alicia arrived and strolled back to the kitchen where she draped her coat over a chair. Then she headed for the master bedroom where Amber was on her knees servicing Sam.

"You guys started the party without me." Alicia pretended to pout, but she was she winking at them playfully.

Sam smiled, showing his bad teeth. "Amber said you got us some specials oils. What ya' got?"

"Sure do, honey, but we're saving that for later. You're going to be here for a while so we want to take our time." Alicia turned on some exotic music, dancing and slowly removing her clothes, one piece at a time. "Amber and I will take you to paradise."

Sam held up his empty glass. "I want another drink."

"We'll keep your glass full, sweetheart. Don't you worry," Alicia headed back to the kitchen. "It's too early," she whispered to Amber as she left. "We'll have some fun first."

"Yes, we have plenty of time," Amber said.

Alicia filled his glass with mostly whiskey and added a splash of Coca-Cola. When Alicia returned to the bedroom, Amber was on her knees again.

"Hey, guys. Lets all get naked—we can really enjoy ourselves." Alicia slipped off her bra. Together, the sisters helped Sam remove his clothes and draped his pants over a chair.

"Lie down, Sam. I'm going to take my panties off and sit on your face," Amber said.

"And I'm going to continue where Amber left off," Alicia said.

"You girls sure know how to please a man," Sam murmured and moaned, with Amber's hairless crotch resting on his face.

They continued through the evening. The sisters were making sure that Sam would have more to drink than he should.

Alicia slid off Sam and went back to the kitchen. Now was the time for the special pill. She put the small pill into his glass, added the whiskey and Coke, and returned to the bedroom.

"You guys, let's take a time out. We'll catch up on our drinking." She handed Sam his drink.

"Bottoms up." Alicia said and they clinked glasses.

Within forty minutes, Sam was out like a light. The girls searched through his wallet and found $2000. They continued going through the wallet for anything else that would be of value.

"Look at this!" Amber said. "He has three driver's licenses—two from Illinois and one from Florida."

"So?" Alicia replied.

"Two of them have a different name. It's Manny Bruso, but the picture is the same."

Alicia sighed. "Big deal. He probably uses them for his work."

The girls dressed him and found his car keys in his coat pocket. In the darkness, they dragged his unconscious body out to his car and placed him in the passenger seat.

"I'll drive his car and you follow me," Alicia said.

"Where are you taking him?"

"The honky-tonk on Main Street in Marinette. I think it's called The Rusty Horn."

"Then what?" Amber asked.

"We'll park in the back and then shove him into the driver's seat. Then we'll get the hell out of there."

"Yeah, if he calls us later, we'll just tell him that he paid us two grand after we finished partying and drove away." Amber was smiling. "We can say we were worried about him driving because he was pretty drunk."

"I doubt if we'll ever hear from Sam or Manny or

whatever his name is again," Alicia said, looking at the two grand they had made for just a few hours work.

Manny slowly opened his eyes, but everything was blurry. He had a hell of a headache too. He had no idea where he was or how he'd gotten there. He opened the driver's door and the inside lights came on. Looking at his watch, he squinted, trying to concentrate. It appeared to be 4:17 in the morning. He reeked of booze and smelled of sex. The last thing he remembered was partying with the girls. There weren't any other cars in the parking lot, just his. Manny got out and stumbled around trying to get his legs underneath him. He reached for his wallet—the money he'd had with him earlier was gone. *What the fuck's happened?*

He pulled out onto Main Street and turned right. After several blocks he still wasn't sure where he was. After turning around, he drove the opposite direction. He recognized the Marinette Marina on his right. A mile later he pulled into the space at his motel room. Manny reached into the glove box and retrieved his room key.

He stumbled to the door and went inside, crossed to the small refrigerator, and grabbed a bottle of beer. *A little hair of the dog that bit me,* he thought. He collapsed on the bed and fell asleep.

25

Monday morning, when Cole was at his desk, catching up on what happened over the weekend, the phone rang. "Cole Dominic," he answered.

"Hi, Officer Dominic. It's Punky. Can I come over in an hour?"

"Sure, I'll be here."

Punky didn't own a car anymore; he'd had to sell it for cash once when he was really broke. His only mode of transportation was his bicycle. Cole glanced out the window; it looked like it could rain any minute. He returned to the papers on his desk.

"Hey, Cole. There's a guy up front who says he has an appointment with you. Says his name is Punky," an officer called back to him.

"Send him in," Cole said.

An officer escorted Punky to where Cole was seated at his desk. He was pale; he looked as though he had not eaten lately. As for his grooming, he hadn't shaven for several days; his jeans were filthy as was the faded Green Bay Packers tee shirt.

"Hello, Punky," Cole greeted him warmly.

Punky nodded and took the seat across from Cole.

"Would you like something to eat or drink?"

"I'm kinda hungry." Punky was staring at the donuts on the desk beside them.

Cole reached for the box. "Help yourself."

Punky had consumed three donuts and was about to have another when Cole slid the box away.

"Do you have any news for me?" Cole asked.

Punky eased back in his chair. "A little."

"Let's hear it," Cole said.

"Can we talk in private?"

"Yeah, follow me." Cole led the way to an empty interview room, turned on the lights, and closed the door behind them. "Okay, what do you have?"

"Can you protect me?"

"Protect you from what?" Cole replied.

"From Sam. He scares me," Punky said at last.

"Okay, you can be my CI," Cole said.

"What's a CI?"

"A confidential informant," Cole answered.

"Confidential, huh?" Punky said.

"Yeah, yeah. Now what the hell do you have for me?"

"Well, me and my buddies went out for a few beers last night. We went to that country place, on Main Street. You know the one."

"Yes. The Rusty Horn"

"Yeah. That's it."

Cole was becoming frustrated. "Damn, Punky, get to the point."

"Yeah, okay. Well, we closed the place up and when we left there was a red Camaro parked in the back."

Cole's interest increased. "Did you get the license number?"

"No, I took off runnin' down the street."

"Why?"

"I thought Sam was waiting for me in his car, and he was going to hurt me. I was scared, Mr. Dominic."

"Okay, Punky. If you see the car again, wait until Sam isn't around and get the plate number and call me. Can you do that?"

"Yeah, I will if I see it."

Cole walked Punky to the front of the station. It was raining. "Come on, Punky, we'll put your bike in the back of my pick up, and I'll take you home."

26

Manny slept most of the day. Maid service had knocked twice and each time he told them to leave him alone. The room was a mess, and he needed a shower badly. His head was pounding.

What the fuck went on last night? He opened his wallet again: all the money was gone. *Did the twins steal it?*

He reached for his cell phone and entered Amber's number. There was no answer. Manny reached behind the headboard of the bed, where he had taped several envelopes with various amounts of cash in them. He picked one, took out a thousand, and placed it in his wallet.

Manny knew he was a mess; he decided to shower and clean up. When he was finished, he ordered a pizza to be delivered within thirty minutes. Perhaps if he had some food the headache would go away.

After he'd finished the pizza, he tried Amber again. Still no answer. This time he left a message to call him back, but he didn't say please. "You'd better call me!" He shouted into the phone.

~

Amber stared at the message. "Maybe we should call him and smooth this situation over."

"I agree. I'm sure he has a lot of questions," Alicia said.

Manny's cell rang back; the display showed that it was Amber.

"It's about time you called me," he said angrily.

"I'm sorry, sweetie. I was at the market shopping for groceries and left my phone at home."

"I want to know what happened last night!" he demanded.

"We all had a great time," she said.

"How much did you charge me?"

"We told you it was $1500 and you gave us a $500 tip. We said it was too much, but you insisted." Amber lowered her voice, sultrier than before. "You're just such a sweet and generous guy."

"That doesn't sound like something I'd do," Manny muttered.

"You were really drunk," Amber said. "And we were so very worried about you driving too."

"I've been drunk before.... Nothing like this has ever happened to me."

"What can I say, darlin'? It is what it is," she said.

"I'm not sure I believe you." Manny hung up.

In his own mind, Manny knew that the twins had somehow robbed him, but he had other business to consider first. He would tend to them later, after he'd taken care of the other two. That should certainly put the city into a panic. They'd think there was a serial killer in their midst, and he'd be long gone.

Manny decided it was time to move to another motel again. As he had before, he would search for a new place before he checked out of his current location. Peshtigo was a small community four miles west of Marinette where there were several motels to choose from. Peshtigo was still close enough to his targets that it wouldn't matter.

When Manny stopped for gas, he stepped inside to chat with the lone service station attendant. "Hi. Can you recommend a good motel in Peshtigo?"

"Sure can. My brother-in-law manages a place called the Gray Fox Motor Inn. Decent prices and clean rooms. It's on Route 41, but I don't know the exact address," the young man told him.

"Thanks," Manny said. "And how about a place I can get breakfast?"

"Just down the street. On the right is Mama Jo's—they've got great pancakes."

Manny walked into Mama Jo's and took a seat in a booth. The place was medium-sized and half the tables were filled. Animal heads and deer racks were mounted on the walls. He gathered the owner must be an avid hunter.

He heard laughter coming from a booth at the other end where a group of guys were seated. One he recognized. It was the guy he'd hired to spray-paint the attorney's yacht. The guy was getting up to use the restroom.

Manny left before the waitress could take his order. He couldn't take a chance being seen. The spray-paint punk was looking out into the parking lot as Manny peeled out of the parking lot. A red Camaro stood out like a sore thumb in this community.

27

Kory's phone buzzed on the desk where she was working at her computer. "Hello?" she answered.

"Miss Sims, this is Cora Gibbons, at the Royal Palms. Your grandfather has had a heart attack. It looks serious and the ambulance is on its way. It'll be best if you meet him at Bay Area Medical Center. He should arrive within ten minutes. The hospital is located at Shore Drive and Cheri Boulevard."

"Oh, my God! I'm leaving right now." Kory hung up and grabbed her purse.

She arrived as two different ambulances were pulling into the emergency bays. She found a parking place and ran to the entrance. Her grandfather was on a gurney. He was hooked up to monitors and other devices and was being wheeled into the ER. The doors closed, and she was not allowed in. One of the staff guided her to the waiting room. Kory collapsed in a chair, trying to catch her breath, and phoned Scott. Her heart was racing so fast she wondered whether she was having a heart attack too.

"Hi, honey. How's your day going?" he said. "I miss you."

"I'm at the hospital with Papa. He's had a heart attack," she managed to say between sobs.

"Oh, sweetheart, I'm so sorry. I'll be right there."

Moments later Scott walked into the ER. He rushed to her side and took her in his arms, holding her close. Kory couldn't control her crying.

She gripped Scott's arm. "He can't die—he's all I have left." Every time a nurse passed by, she was sure it must have something to do with her "Papa."

Finally, a nurse dressed in green scrubs emerged from the emergency room. "Miss Sims, we're trying to stabilize him at this time. When he's more stable, we'll move him to ICU. However, he'll probably still be unconscious. If you go into his room, try not to disturb him. He's very weak."

"But... But is he going to be all right?" Kory asked.

"He'll be here in the hospital for at least four or five days. When he goes home, he'll need home nursing care for several weeks," the nurse said.

"Will we see his doctor?" Kory asked.

"Yes, he'll come out and talk with you shortly," the nurse replied.

And for the time, that was that. There was nothing Kory could do.

Oh, hospitals! I thought. I had my own share of terrible memories associated with these places.

Kory wanted to visit the hospital's chapel, and she asked me to accompany her. We returned to the waiting room an hour later. Kory was taking this very hard.

A doctor finally came out to talk to us. "Your grandfather Mr. Sims is on his way to ICU. He's still in critical condition but stable for the moment."

"Can I see him now?" she asked anxiously.

"No visitors for at least three hours, then we'll see after that." The doctor turned and left.

I walked Kory to the cafeteria. We had coffee and a Danish, although she couldn't eat hers. She finally broke down and cried, as if her tears would never stop.

"He has me, and I have him. What will I do if he dies?"

"You have me, sweetheart," I whispered.

"I know," she said, her voice small and pained.

The three hours passed slowly, and then we were allowed to go to his room. Kory's grandfather was unconscious and unresponsive, connected to a new set of monitors. We sat there in silence. His breathing machine was making a soft clicking noise, and the display numbers on a monitor were constantly changing.

Suddenly an alarm beeped, loud and shrill. A red light blinked nonstop. Overhead, the announcement could be heard: "Code Blue. Code Blue." Within seconds the room was filled with nurses, doctors, and staff.

The next thing we knew, we were being ushered out to the waiting area again.

"What happened?" Kory asked.

"He's having another heart attack," the nurse told her.

"Oh, my God!" Kory screamed. "No!"

Thirty minutes passed; a doctor came into the ICU waiting room. "I'm so very sorry, Miss Sims. He didn't make it. We did everything we could to save him."

Kory collapsed and fell to the floor. The doctor reacted immediately. He pulled something from the pocket of his white lab coat, snapped a capsule of ammonia smelling salts, and held it under her nose. She jerked back her head, opened her eyes, and began crying again.

Sometime later, I drove her to my place. I carried her from the Jeep upstairs to my bedroom. While she was getting in bed I went downstairs to the liquor cabinet and grabbed a bottle of Jack Daniels and two glasses.

We both needed something to calm our nerves. Kory was exhausted and soon fell asleep.

I took the bottle of bourbon and went to one of the spare bedrooms. I started thinking of how I could help her with the arrangements for her grandfather. I wondered whether he had a will or living trust.

I called the hospital. As her attorney, I asked them to release the body to our local funeral home. "Could you send the original death certificate to my office?" Kory had never spoken about her papa's requests. Had he wanted a burial or a cremation? I would ask her tomorrow.

Kory had left her papa's house so quickly, I wondered whether she'd remembered to lock up. I decided to drive over and check it out. I circled the house, rattling and testing each door, and everything seemed secure. Walking back to my car, I noticed a Camaro with Illinois plates rolling past her house. It was too dark to tell if it was red. I tried to catch up to him, but my Jeep was no match for a Camaro. At least I knew he was still in town. I headed back to my place, feeling more than a little on edge.

Manny had driven back to his motel. He was sure that both Punky and the attorney had gotten a good look at his car. He dialed Mo's cell phone.

"Hey, Manny!" Mo said.

"Boss, you need to send me another car. This time make it an older, nondescript model. This should be the last one," Manny said.

"It had better be," Mo growled at him. "Okay. Tomorrow, same place, same time."

Manny started reviewing the timing for the next day. He'd need to check out of his present dump about noon and then meet Mo's guy at three, before checking in at the Gray Fox Motor Inn in Peshtigo with his new ride.

28

Simone had asked for an extra day off. She deserved it, after house sitting and taking care of K9 too. So it was just Kory and me at home. I was in the kitchen fixing breakfast when Kory stumbled downstairs dressed in a pair of my pajamas.

I stared at her appreciatively. Although she looked terribly sad, she still was a lovely sight. "Would you like a serving of my world famous flapjacks?"

"No thanks. Nothing but some coffee with a shot of that brandy."

"Coming up," I said.

Her eyes were red and swollen. I was sure she had slept very little last night. She must have a hard time believing her papa was gone.

We talked very little. I told her what I had taken care of while she slept. She seemed to accept and approve, but she did not respond. She just sat staring into space and sipped on the lightly spiked coffee.

"You'll probably need to go over to The Royal Palms and retrieve your grandfather's personal effects. And, troublesome as it is, you might need to settle with them today too. I'll go with you if you want me to." I'd been holding her hand ever since we sat down together.

"Papa said his will is in his safety deposit box at the bank. He'd also expressed his wishes to be cremated...." She gulped back her tears. "He wants his ashes scattered on the Menominee River. I'll need to write his obituary for the paper. And I should have a memorial service too, for all his friends," Kory said.

Sad as her duties were, I wanted to be there for her. I was relieved that she was a signatory on his safety deposit box and that his affairs were in order. Legal troubles can make the loss of a loved one seem that much worse.

Mr. Sims had lived in the Twin Cities all his life. His good neighbors Lee and Joe Balsis prepared refreshments for a reception at their home. "We want to celebrate his life, dear," they told Kory. They had helped her choose photographs of her dear "Papa" and placed them around the house: in the living room, on the piano, on the sideboard, and even down the buffet table. The house was filled with the many cards Kory received. The line seemed endless as cars circled several city blocks, searching for a parking place. His many friends wanted to pay their respects and share the time with Kory.

After his memorial service was over, we took his ashes aboard the *Snow Flake* and proceeded slowly to the center of the river, headed to where the mouth met the bay. Kory let her papa's ashes drift onto the water very, very slowly as though she didn't want to let him go.

Manny met Mo's guy at the bus station; he was right on time. He had brought a 1999 white Ford Taurus that had seen more than a few rough winters. The rocker panels were rusting out, and there were several dents on the driver's side.

Perfect! Manny thought.

They made the exchange, and Mo's guy headed back toward Chicago, while Manny headed for his new digs at the Gray Fox Motor Inn. He checked into the motel and paid for two weeks in advance.

Manny spoke to the manager. "I'll strip my own bed when I needed clean sheets, if that's okay with you. I'll leave them by the door along with any other linens I need." He didn't want the motel staff in his room without him being there.

The manager looked puzzled. "If that's what you want," he said. "Seems a bit strange, though."

After he moved in, Manny went about securing envelopes of cash to the back of the bed headboard. Feeling more secure, he was certain the new location and a different car would make it more difficult for anyone trying to find him.

Manny couldn't get the twins out of his mind. He was sure they had drugged him and helped themselves to all the cash he had on him at the time. Within a couple of weeks, he should be done with the attorney and his girlfriend. He could kill the twins now and make them disappear. They were nobody important. Folks would think they just took off someplace, but he must plan his move very carefully.

He started making a list: duct tape, rope, latex gloves, shovel, measuring tape, heavy plastic drop cloth, large rubber boots, a couple of fifty pound sacks of lye, safety goggles, and a respirator mask.

Then he would need to find a burial site that was out of the way, preferably in the woods. There he would dig two graves, three feet by five feet and about four feet deep. He would need to complete them prior to killing the girls. If he stole a van, he could use it to transport the bodies and then his tire tracks would not be found in the woods, should the bodies be discovered sooner than he'd planned.

He chuckled, smiling to himself. "Now I'll contact the girls for our final get together." He was quite proud of himself, after countless years and so many murders. He had never been caught or even questioned as a suspect in any of them. The twins would be number ten and eleven. The majority of his contracts had been in the Chicago area.

Much as I would miss her, Kory was going back to Sheboygan for a few days.

"I need to be alone for a little while," she told me.

I understood. "You'll be coming back though, won't you?"

"Yes, but I need a break… time to sort things out," she answered. "Even though Papa's affairs were in order, there's still a lot to take care of."

Although I didn't handle many wills and estate matters any more, I understood there was a ton of final bureaucratic tedium ahead for her.

"I'll miss you. I'll be counting the hours until your return, sweetheart." I whispered in her ear, "I love you, Kory."

"And I, you. You're my knight in shinning armor."

We kissed and as she left, I noticed there were tears in her eyes. There was an empty ache in my heart.

29

Manny called Amber and left a message: "Hey, girls, it's me. It's Friday now. I've finished my work in the area, and I'll be leaving in two days. Could we get together one last time before I go? I've bought something special for each of you. I'd like to show my appreciation for treating me to so many exciting times."

He left the motel, headed to Mama Joe's for dinner where only a few cars were parked out front. At nearly seven, he figured the dinner crowd was over; it should be relatively safe to go in. The scents of good food cooking filled the diner. He took a seat with his back to the wall in a location that would allow him to see anyone entering. The special on the menu board was their freshly baked meatloaf with all the trimmings.

"I'll have the special and iced tea," he told the waitress. After she'd thanked him and left, Manny's phone buzzed. *Good!* It was Amber returning his call.

"Hi, Amber." He forced his voice to stay cheerful. This was working out like he'd planned.

"Hi, lover." She always sounded sultry and teasing.

"When can we all get together?"

"You're a real horn-dog, aren't you, Sam?"

He laughed. "You girls make me that way."

"How about tomorrow at our place, around eight." She blew kissing sounds into the phone.

"Perfect. Will $300 each be okay?" he asked.

"Sounds good, unless you want something extra kinky," Amber said.

"See ya' at eight." He clicked off.

His dinner arrived and he ate. Damn, they made a good meatloaf. Maybe everything tasted extra good because his plans were falling in place.

Manny left the restaurant and cruised around downtown Marinette. He'd spotted a white delivery van parked behind a bakery next to the Holiday Inn. He pulled around, parked in the hotel's parking lot, and walked to where the white van had been left. Peering through the driver's window, he was shocked and pleased to discover they had left the keys in the ignition and the doors were unlocked. Certain small, old towns evidently still would do that sort of thing; it certainly made his plans even easier.

It was Friday night at The Oar House, and this guy was trying to hit on Amber. He hadn't needed to ask for her name. Everyone there seemed to know her.

"Hi, Amber," he said. "I'm Punky."

Amber let him buy her a couple of drinks. But when she left, he'd followed her out to her car. She turned around. "Punky, you're a nice enough guy, but not my type. And you really can't afford me. See ya' around." Driving away, she'd smiled and waved to him, although she'd found him rather creepy.

Manny had gone to several stores to purchase the various items on his list, trying to avoid the cameras in each place. When he got back to the motel, he put everything in one bag except the boots, shovels, and the two heavy bags of lye.

By Saturday morning he had found the perfect spot to dig the twins' graves. He scraped at the ground with a shovel, removing the fallen leaves and debris from where he would be piling the dirt. He measured out the side by side graves and started digging. Two hours later he was finished. He stood back, admiring his work; it looked pretty good. "Later tonight, the twins will be resting here for eternity," he said out loud for the woods to hear.

All the work had made him hungry. He stopped at a fast food burger joint for lunch. On his way home he stopped at a liquor store and picked up a couple of six packs and a fifth of whiskey. The rest of the afternoon he spent lying by the pool and drinking beer.

Manny double-checked to make sure he had everything he needed and finished loading his car. At around a quarter past seven, Manny pulled away from the motel and headed to the hotel parking lot. He found a spot close to the rear of the bakery, parked, and walked over to the van.

Manny got in and fumbled the keys into the ignition. After starting the engine, he checked the gas gauge: it was half full. He drove around to where he had parked his car and transferred all the equipment into the van. Satisfied, he started toward the twins' house.

It was 7:50 when he arrived and just starting to get dark. There were lights on inside the house, but the porch light was off. That was good: it made the delivery van less obvious. Manny walked up the front steps and rang the doorbell.

Amber answered the door. She was wearing a scarlet red teddy and holding a bottle of beer. "Come in, sweetie." She handed him the icy cold bottle.

He looked her over from head to toe, liking what he saw. "That's a great outfit."

"Just for you, darlin'," she said.

"Is Alicia here?" Manny asked.

Alicia came into the room to greet him. She was wearing an identical teddy, but it was white. "I'm right here."

"We wanted to wear something really special for you, since it's your last time here," Amber said.

It's the last thing you'll ever wear, Manny was thinking.

Alicia turned on music that was low and sensual. "Let's get started," she said.

They took turns undressing Manny. Once he was naked, Amber led him to a straight-backed chair. "Here, you sit down." She eased down on him, giving him a lap dance. Alicia stood behind him, reaching over to caress his chest with her special oils.

The combination must have been working; Manny was hard as a rock.

Amber was stroking his penis, teasing him. "What would you like now?" she cooed.

"How about you both go over to the bed and lean over—like with your butts high in the air," Manny suggested.

"Okay," Alicia said.

Amber was giggling. "Is this about right?"

"Perfect!" Manny walked over to them and unsnapped their teddies. He reached between Amber's legs and then Alicia's, rubbing deep against their clean-shaven pussies.

"Use some of the oil—over there on the night stand," Alicia said.

"Okay," Manny said. He applied the oil to all three of them. He begin fucking them moving from one to the other, and soon he exploded inside Amber.

"What now?" Alicia asked.

Manny gasped and sighed. "Give me time to recover." He collapsed onto the chair.

"I think I know what will help," Amber said.

"What?" Manny asked.

"How about my sister and I do our thing together?" she said.

"Take your pretty teddies off first." He began stroking himself and watched. It was just as he had planned it. The thought of killing them was arousing him even more.

"I want you girls to sixty-nine each other, with Amber on top. That will help me get ready," he said.

The twins did as he asked. Several minutes later Manny stood and crossed the room to Amber. He gently raised her head, putting one hand on her forehead and the other on the back of her head, and then with a quick jerk he snapped her neck, killing her instantly and without a sound.

The weight of Amber's body was fully on Alicia; she was pinned down. "What happened?"

They were her last words. Manny snapped her neck too. He stepped back and admired his work. *What a beautiful picture,* he thought.

Manny slipped back into his clothes. He went outside to the van, bringing back the gloves, duct tape, rope, and two drop cloths. He put on the latex gloves, but first grabbed the beer bottle he had drunk from, washed it off, and tossed it into their garbage can. Back at the bed, where the two girls were still sprawled, he rolled Amber's body to one side of the bed. He tied their hands and feet so it would be easier to roll them into the drop cloth and carry them to the van.

Manny checked out the side door to see if anyone was around, then backed the van into the driveway until it was beside the side door. Back inside, he placed the drop cloth beside the bed and rolled Alicia's body off and onto the drop cloth. He rolled her up and taped the cloth shut. He carried her out and slid her into the van.

Next it was Amber's turn. He returned to the house once more and searched through their purses until he'd retrieved the $1500 in cash, then he picked up both teddies as a remembrance. He shut off all the lights and left. It was fully dark now, just moonlight and a few stars.

He drove directly to the graves he'd dug in the woods. It was a quarter of a mile from the nearest paved road. Manny parked the van and shut off the headlights, leaving the parking lights on directed at the two graves. He was certain that the woods were dense enough that a small amount of light would not be seen. He carried the girls to the graves and opened the plastic drop cloths, lowered each into her own space. Last, he put on the safety goggles and respirator mask, before pouring lye over them until their bodies were thoroughly covered. He shoveled the dirt back in so that each grave had a slight mound. He smacked the dirt with his shovel so they were level and then covered them with the leaves and debris he'd set aside. Everything looked natural and undisturbed.

He turned back onto the paved road and drove to the bakery to park the van where he'd found it. He returned to the motel in his 1999 Ford. Once there, he locked the door and pulled out two teddies—one red, one white. Holding his two souvenirs, he began masturbating.

The driver who handled deliveries for the bakery arrived at work Monday morning. After opening the van, he noticed the mileage he'd recorded in his logbook Friday afternoon wasn't the same. Twenty-eight additional miles showed on the odometer. He mentioned the discrepancy to his boss. "Someone must have taken it for a joy ride over the weekend," his boss said. "After this, lock the van at night and leave the keys inside the bakery." The driver readily agreed.

30

I was finding it difficult not talking to Kory, and this was only the second day since she'd left for Sheboygan. I'd been tempted to call her, but I knew she needed private time right now. I forced myself to wait; maybe she'd call me later.

My cell phone buzzed; the caller ID showed it was Cole. "Hey, partner. What's up?" I said.

"Just want to let you know we have a new missing persons case."

"Don't you mean 'person'?" I asked.

"No, *persons,*" Cole replied.

"Tell me about it," I said.

"It's two women, twin sisters living in Menominee. You're aware we share cases of this nature, aren't you?"

"Of course. When was it reported?" I asked.

"Sunday morning. However, you know we always wait about two days before we get involved," Cole said.

"Any clues?" I asked.

"Nope, the house was checked out by Menominee PD. The girls' cars were in the garage. The house was locked up, but their father had a key. Inside everything was fine except the bed was a mess and a straight-backed chair was in the middle of the room facing the bed. Even their purses were still there. No signs of foul play though."

"How old are the sisters?"

"Twenty-eight. From the pictures I've seen they're quite pretty."

"Kids?"

"No, neither one. They're both single."

"They'll probably show up, wondering what all the fuss is about. They're most likely out with their friends," I said.

"Maybe." Cole sounded doubtful.

"Has the father been helpful?" I asked.

"He owns the house and rents it to the girls. The only time he sees them is when the rent's due and he stops by. Otherwise he doesn't have much contact with them," Cole replied.

"What bothers me is that wherever they've gone, they didn't take their purses. How often do you see women without purses?" I asked.

"Yeah, I know. Talk to you tomorrow." Cole clicked off.

Kory was calling me. I set aside my work and answered. "Hi, sweetie, how is everything?" I asked, relieved to hear her voice.

"I hate to bother you, but I have a problem," she said. Her voice was trembling.

"Can I help?"

"I hope so," she said, but she sounded frustrated.

"Will you tell me what's bothering you?"

"It's not what... it's who!" she exclaimed.

"A person?"

"Yes. Do you remember Bernie Sandowski, the guy here in Sheboygan? Well he's back. Somehow he's found out I'm here in town. He's been calling me at all hours of the night and leaving godawful messages and threatening me.

"I guess he didn't get the message the first time," I said.

She was starting to cry. "I'm scared of him."

"Where does he hang out?" I asked.

"You're not going to do anything rash, are you?"

"No, don't worry. I promise he won't bother you any longer. Just tell me where he can be found."

"He owns an auto body shop on South Kendall Street. I'll get you the address."

"Not necessary. I just need the business name."

"Sandowski Auto Body Repair. Pretty original, huh?" she answered.

"I'll need a description of him—for my friend."

"Oh... five-ten, wavy black hair, and about one-ninety. He has a tattoo of a skunk on his left forearm."

"Sounds charming," I said. "I'll make a few calls."

"Please don't get in any trouble," she begged.

"Someone will visit him and hopefully show him the errors of his ways."

"I love you, Scott. I know you'll always be there to protect me."

"I love you too, sweetheart. Will you be coming home soon?"

"In a few days," she answered.

"Take all the time you need. I'll be waiting for you."

"Bye for now," she whispered and hung up.

I didn't have any intentions of calling anyone else to help out. I wanted to handle this problem by myself. I knew better legally than to put hands on this guy, but the anger in me took over. He was messing with the woman I loved, and I'm wouldn't stand for it.

I called Cole and asked him to watch my place for the couple of days. I told him I'd be out of town. Without asking any questions, he agreed. Last, I left Simone a note.

I didn't have any particular plan in mind about what I would do. The first day I'd check him out and follow him around. The next day, I'd make a decision on how to get my message across. From past experience, I'd learned that talking to guys like this had no effect. They only understand acts of violence. I slipped into old clothes, remembering to bring a winter ski mask and a pair of thin, black leather gloves. I jumped into the Jeep and headed for Sheboygan.

31

On my way, I put the information into my GPS and—*voilà*—my route to Bernie's business was on display. After passing Green Bay, the traffic was light. Driving southeast on Highway 43, the sprawling farmlands appeared on both sides of the road. Wisconsin is a truly beautiful and scenic state; it almost made me forget what awaited me ahead.

The driving time from my house to Mr. Sandowski's auto repair business was two and a half hours. The business appeared run down and poorly taken care of. There was a bright red Ford 250 pickup parked in an area marked "Reserved." I would have taken bets and given good odds that it belonged to Mr. Sandowski. The Wisconsin plate read: AUTO MAN.

I parked across the street from the building and waited. Forty minutes went by before a man came out. He fit the description that Kory had given me to a tee. As he drove away, I slipped in behind him, staying about half a block back. We worked our way across town and ended up in a location that was somewhat familiar to me: it was where Kory lived. The red pickup stopped about a block down the street from Kory's home. The driver remained in the vehicle and appeared to be on his cell phone. I was using my binoculars to observe him: when he finished the call, he drove away.

I punched in Kory's number and she picked up immediately. "Did you just receive a call from Mr. Sandowski?" I asked before she could say anything.

"Yes! How did you know? Are you close by?" She sounded near panic.

"Yes. I'm pulling into your driveway as we speak," I said.

"Come in the side door." She clicked off.

As Kory requested I came in using the side entrance. She was sitting at the kitchen table, visibly shaken.

"What's happening?" she asked.

I told her what I had done since arriving in Sheboygan. "Do you think he'll call you again tonight?"

"No, I don't think so," she said.

"Okay, I have a plan."

"What do you mean? A plan—a plan for what?"

"A plan to keep you safe and stop this asshole from ever bothering you again." I hesitated, but only a moment. "I want you to call him. Tell him to stop bothering you and never come around your home again."

"Why would I do that? I don't even want to talk to him. I hate the son of bitch."

"If you tell a guy like him *not* to do something, that's exactly what he will do. Do you have any weapons in the house?"

"No, the only weapon I have is an old Louisville Slugger bat I keep in the closet," she said.

"That's perfect. After I get my stuff from my car, you take my Jeep and find a motel for the night. I'll stay here to greet Mr. Sandowski when he arrives."

She looked puzzled. "Then what?"

"He and I will have a brief discussion." I put my arms around her; just feeling her close to me was reassuring.

Kory gathered up what she would need for her stay at the motel, loaded the Jeep, and came back into the house. She made the call to Bernie, told him what we had rehearsed, and then hung up.

"Before you leave, give me your car keys," I said.

Then she was gone.

As it got dark, I turned off all the lights except for two nightlights. Waiting, I began to wonder. Could this guy possibly be the one who had been giving me so much grief over the last two months?

I stepped outside onto the front porch; there was a full view of the street from both directions. Even if Bernie parked a hundred yards away, I could still see his headlights. Kory's car was in the driveway and nothing looked suspicious. Since the house was dark, he might believe she had gone to bed. It was nearing ten o'clock when a vehicle appeared, moving slowly along the darkened street with only its parking lights on.

I put the ski mask over my head; it covered my face except for two holes for my eyes and a slit for the mouth. After slipping on the leather gloves, I went to the closet, picked up the baseball bat, and stood in the darkest corner of her bedroom to wait. My face began to sweat under the wool ski mask. *Why is it taking him so long?* I wondered.

The side door rattled: he was trying to turn the handle. I had locked it earlier, making sure that he would actually need to break in. The clatter of breaking glass broke the silence. He was inside and creeping quietly through the house, heading toward the bedroom.

Once I was certain he was inside her room, I stepped out and swung the bat low and hard, making contact with his knees. I could hear bones break and feel the vibration through the wooden bat. He fell to the floor screaming in pain. I put my foot on his neck, pinning him to the floor.

Disguising my voice, I said, "You leave her completely alone or next time, I will kill you! Do you understand?"

Sobbing, his face contorted with the excruciating pain, he nodded. "Who the fuck are you?"

"I'm one of the many that don't like you. We're looking out for your worst interests, asshole! Do you want some water?" I asked.

He nodded.

In the kitchen I filled a glass, not really giving a shit whether he was thirsty on not, but I wanted his DNA on the glass, just in case. I pressed the glass to his mouth and he drank. Then I put tape over his mouth and gave his knee a quick squeeze. He jerked with the sharp pain, but I smiled.

He couldn't walk and needed medical attention. I tied his hands behind his back, reached into his pants pocket, and pulled out his truck keys and his cell phone.

"I'll be right back. You be a good boy and stay put," I said and walked down to his truck.

I drove the truck up the street to Kory's house and parked behind her car in the driveway. Back in the bedroom, I picked him up, put him over my shoulder, carried him out to the truck, and then laid him down in the bed of the truck. He was moaning with pain.

"Shut the fuck up!" I said.

He nodded.

"I'll punch in a number for you so you can tell someone where you are, and that you need medical help. If you say anything else, I'll use the bat again. *Capisce?*" I removed the tape and put in the number he gave me and held the phone close to his ear.

"Tony, it's Bernie. I'm hurt and need your help. I'm on Willow Street just past Warren—in my truck. Come quick."

I clicked off and tossed his phone into the cab of the truck. "Remember what I told you, asshole!"

After driving Bernie's truck a block away from Kory's house, I walked back, climbed into her car, and drove away. As I was winding my way back down the hill, headed for downtown, I called Kory.

"Where are you staying?" I asked.

"The Best Western on Noble Street," she answered.

"I'll be there in a few," I said and clicked off, forgetting that she didn't have GPS in her car. I called her again and received the directions. Minutes later I was knocking on her door. She peaked out the curtains to make sure it was me and opened the door.

"Is everything okay?" she asked.

"You bet." I smiled. "It went like clockwork."

"Will there be any trouble?"

"No, I'm sure everything will be fine." It had actually felt good to let out the aggression I had pent up inside me, from the all that had happened to me lately.

"Did you hurt him?" she asked.

"Well, he's on his way to the hospital about now."

"The hospital?"

"Yes, the hospital," I said. And then I told her the story.

"Is my house a total mess?" She asked me.

"No, I made sure everything looks normal. However, you do have a broken window pane in the side door. That can be easily repaired."

We prepared for bed, turned off the lights, and Kory snuggled up to me.

She squeezed my arm. "You're my favorite good guy and bad guy."

"The bad guy only comes out when absolutely necessary," I said.

"I hope I never have to see that side of you again," she whispered.

It was so good to be near her once more, kissing and making love, made all the more special because I needed her and she needed me.

The next morning we drove both cars back to her house.

"Let me go in first to check everything out. You wait here until I tell you it's okay."

I went through the house and nothing seemed out of order.

"I've been thinking," she said, "as long as we have

two cars here, I'm going to fill them with what I really need for a while and take them home."

"Take them home?" I repeated.

"Yes," she said. "Home is where you are."

"Amen," I said.

"I can sell this place and Papa's too," Kory said. "Do you think you could find room for me at your place?"

"You must be a mind reader." I laughed.

When we arrived home, I put Kory's clothes and what else she'd brought with her in a spare bedroom. It was a delight to share my master bath and bed with her.

In one of the spare bedrooms, we arranged a small desk for her computer; there she could work on her manuscript in private. Each morning, we've gone to her computer and checked the Sheboygan newspaper for any reports about Bernie Sandowski. There was nothing.

32

Cole called to tell me that Punky had gotten drunk and was in a bar fight. One of his front teeth was knocked out. Apparently the other guy tossed him out the front door. Punky, in all his wisdom, found a hefty rock about the size of a softball, marched back in, and threw it into the mirror behind the bar. Bottles of booze and glass went flying everywhere. The police were called. Cole's confidential informant Punky had spent the last two days in jail.

To make things worse the Menominee police were listing him as a person of interest in the case of the twin girls who had gone missing. They had a video of him leaving a tavern with Amber the night before she was reported missing.

In the state of Wisconsin, it is suggested that attorneys contribute up to fifty hours a year of pro bono work. I usually give my time to charitable organizations, at a much reduced rate and occasionally for free. However, I believed that Punky was in need of legal counsel right now. I would devote my time to him at no charge. Although it would count toward my pro bono work, each of us would benefit. At least, I hoped.

I began by having Punky released from jail and paying his bail of $500. The tavern owner's insurance estimate for cost of repairs and merchandise totaled $5,000. Punky, of course, was dead broke. I negotiated with the tavern owner to let Punky make payments of $100 a week for the owner's loss of business. The owner said the repairs would take two weeks. The amount they settled on was $2,000, to be paid in full at the end of five months. The court was happy with the arrangement and agreed to monitor it until fully paid.

I've hired Punky to take care of my landscaping and do odd the jobs that would come up around my old house. Furthermore, he'll be shoveling my driveway and sidewalks in the winter. And Punky has also found a job at one of the manufacturing companies along the river.

A week had passed since Manny had buried the twins. He decided to do a drive-by, just for old times' sake, he told himself. Pulling off the paved road, he noticed several pieces of heavy construction equipment parked in the area. He didn't want to make contact with the equipment operators. He slammed his car into reverse, backed out to the paved road, and sped away.

His natural instinct was to flee, and as far away as possible. However, Manny had made a commitment to Mo and been paid a large sum of money in advance. There was more to come later, when the contract was completed. If he reneged on the deal, he knew his days as a hit man would be over. And Mo would hunt him down and kill him.

Manny drove back to the motel in Peshtigo. He sat on the edge of his bed staring at a blank TV screen as though he were in a trance. Now he needed to get a plan together about what to do with the attorney and his squeeze.

~

Kory had contacted a real estate agent in Sheboygan and made an appointment to meet with her at the house concerning listing it for sale. Later in the afternoon of the same day she'd contracted with a moving company, scheduled to pack all her belongings, and move them to a storage unit in Marinette. A few days later everything was completed.

Kory posted a *For Sale by Owner* sign in front of her grandfather's house. Scott could help her with the paperwork, if there was an offer, and she'd save the commission fee. She also posted an ad in the local paper and scheduled the ad to run for two weeks.

She'd been working on her computer when her cell phone buzzed. "Hello?"

"Hi, Kory. It's Beth. I haven't had much time lately. How about lunch this Friday?"

"Day after tomorrow?"

"Yes," Beth said.

"Sounds great for me. Where and what time?" Kory said.

"We could meet at The Crew's Quarters at noon."

"It's a date," Kory said. They both clicked off.

Kory called her real estate agent in Sheboygan. "Good morning, Gail."

"Good morning to you too, Kory. I'm glad you called. I'll be holding an open house this weekend at your place. Have there been any changes concerning the listing?"

"Only that I want to make sure that for any offer we receive, the buyer must be qualified and preferably they don't have any contingencies. I'd really appreciate a fairly quick closing."

"That's understood," Gail said.

"Good luck." Kory hung up feeling satisfied with the progress being made.

33

Marinette's city limits extended far beyond the small downtown area, possibly taking into account any chance of future expansion. In the city's rural area, a local contractor had hired a surveying team to stake out a twenty-acre parcel of land he had purchased few weeks ago.

Today, the heavy equipment operators had begun work, clearing a portion of the land for a new road that would lead from the county's paved road to the first of three model homes for his new development.

During the process, a bulldozer had unearthed two bodies. Work stopped immediately, and the contractor dialed 911. A dispatcher took the information and relayed it to the Marinette Police. She asked the contractor to stay away from the scene and to not contaminate it.

Cole and four other units were dispatched to the location, arriving at about the same time. Cole ordered crime scene tape to be put up a distance from where one of the bodies was still half resting in the large scoop of the bulldozer. The other body was on the ground mixed in with fresh dirt. One bare foot was visible but seemed distorted.

After accessing the scene, Cole called his chief. "Sir, this appears to be above our level of investigation. Would you please call the state police for their assistance? Have them send a forensic team. I'll keep the site sanitized until they arrive."

After his call ended, Cole began taking pictures from outside the taped area using a telephoto lens. There seemed to be a white slimy residue covering most of the body along with a heavy plastic sheet hanging off to one side of the dozer's scoop.

He called to one of his officers. "Go back to the paved road and block the entrance. Don't allow anyone other than the state police to enter, especially the press, and keep your emergency lights off." He didn't worry about helicopters. The local news groups were so small none could afford one. If a chopper did appear, it would be the state police.

The smell of decaying flesh caused the officers to retreat with handkerchiefs covering their faces. While he waited, Cole phoned Scott.

~

I picked up on the first ring. It was Cole. "Hey, partner!"

"I'm not sure yet, but I think we've just found the missing twin sisters."

"Are they okay?"

"Not by a long shot. It was an accidental find. They were dug up by a bulldozer at a construction site," Cole said. "We're waiting for the state's forensic team."

"You've got a lot on your plate now, I know. Will you keep me in the loop?"

"Absolutely," Cole said and hung up.

Dispatch had notified the coroner and medical examiner about the bodies. A vehicle was dispatched to transport the remains to the coroner's office after the forensic team and their photographers had completed their work.

The forensic team arrived by helicopter and methodically set about examining the ground and the bodies. Hundreds of pictures were taken, with markers placed in various locations all around. Body bags were used to secure each of the victims, then placed in the coroner's transportation vehicle before the final stop at the coroner's lab. The state team boarded the helicopter that was quickly airborne and landed noisily behind police station. The state medical examiner had soon joined the coroner at his lab, and they began their work behind closed doors.

So far the press was unaware what was going on, but it would only be a matter of time before the news leaked out. One of the construction gang had called a TV station. A reporter was sent to the crime scene and another to the police station. No one would make any official comment.

The identities of the two women were released to the public, after the police had notified their father. The story appeared in the morning paper with the headline: *Two Local Women Murdered.* The paper included pictures of the pretty identical twins. According to the story, the murdered sisters were discovered buried in a field west of the city and were unearthed accidentally by a construction crew working in the area.

The police had not released any other information, even though they had received the completed report from the two medical examiners. It described how difficult it was to perform the autopsy because of the damage caused by the lye. In the report, the ME had determined that in each case death was caused by suffocation.

In the movies and TV shows, a hulking brute violently snaps a person neck, supposedly killing him or her instantly. In reality it doesn't happen that way. Snapping the head fractures the spine, and paralyzes the person immediately. The severed spinal cord will not allow oxygen to flow, and the person will die of suffocation.

Also, the examiners had found two distinctly identical sets of DNA in each girl. It was from a male, indicating recent sexual activity. The DNA was taken from their vaginas. One indicated only "recent sexual activity," but the other produced actual dead sperm.

I set aside the newspaper with its grim story. Cole had shared the ME's report with me too. Three murders in two months and all the weird stuff that's been happening to me.... What the hell was going on in our small town? Could it all be connected?

My thoughts were echoed by the townspeople. There were an extreme number of calls to the MPD, asking for better protection and more officer visibility. Residents, noticing officers having lunch or dinner, would ask them to get back out on the streets to protect them. I surely didn't envy those cops.

The state forensic team went to the house where the twin sisters had lived, but the only evidence they found was pubic hairs on the bed linen. Tests showed it was from a male with the same DNA as found in the twins. The ME was almost positive the murders had taken place at the twins' house, but there wasn't any match for the male's DNA in the Wisconsin database. They sent the samples to CODIS and hoped for a hit. Whoever it was had never been arrested or committed any crimes in Wisconsin that required a DNA sample. Marinette and Menominee police were stumped.

Manny flipped on the TV at his motel in time for the local news. A news reporter was standing near the crime scene tape in an open field.

"I'm just a few feet away from where the twin sisters were found." She went on with the story of their homicide or at least with what little information they had.

"Fuck!" Manny said. He knew it was inevitable the bodies would be found, but not nearly this quick. *I don't see how they have anything to tie it to me.*

He switched off the TV and started pacing back and forth.

"Shit, that really fucks things up," he said aloud. His hands were sweating and his heart was beating wildly. He got in the shower, and let the cool water cascade over his body, hoping it would calm him down. After ten minutes he got out, dried off, and lay on the bed, staring at the ceiling.

~

Kory greeted Beth at The Crew's Quarters. "Hey, girl! It's been too long." Kory kissed Beth lightly on the cheek, and Beth returned the warm gesture.

"What's new in your life?" Beth asked.

"Sorry to say, it's not good. My grandfather passed away a couple weeks ago."

Beth reached for Kory's hand. "Oh, I'm so sorry."

"He had been quite ill for a long time now."

"Will you be going back to Sheboygan to live?"

Kory decided not to go into details about what had recently happened in Sheboygan. "No. I put my house up for sale, along with Papa's here in Marinette. I've moved in with Scott, at least temporarily."

Beth smiled. "That sounds promising."

"So how have you been?" Kory leaned closer, hoping to hear some good news.

"Well, I've been offered a great job with Northwestern Memorial Hospital in Chicago."

"Are you going to take it?"

"I'm considering it," Beth said, but sounded hesitant.

"What could possibly be holding you back?" Kory asked.

"I've really fallen hard for Cole—I don't want to lose him."

"There's 300 miles between here and Chicago. Long distance relationships are hard to maintain. I know, because I tried it a long time ago and it didn't work," Kory said.

"Damn! It's tearing me up," Beth replied.

"How soon do you have to give them an answer?"

"By next week—and they want me to start right away. I haven't had the nerve to tell Cole yet." Elbows on the table, she held her head in her hands.

"Don't wait too long if you decide to take the job," Kory said. Their lunch arrived and they clinked their wine glasses, toasting their friendship.

That evening, Beth had asked Cole to her apartment for dinner. When he arrived she greeted him with a bottle of cold beer and a warm kiss. She gestured toward the small couch in the front room. "Here, make yourself comfortable."

Something was bothering her; Cole could tell. He decided he would let her bring it up—whatever it was—when she wanted to.

At first Beth was busy in the kitchen; light, casual conversation passed between them. "Dinner's ready," she finally announced. Smiling, she ushered him into the dining area.

Cole joined her at the table. "Wow! It all smells wonderful."

"I hope you like it."

"Beth, I like everything about you," Cole said, warm tenderness in his voice.

Suddenly Beth burst into tears.

"Oh, my God! Beth, what's wrong?"

"I'm sorry, Cole. Please forgive me."

"For what? Did I say something wrong?"

"No, what you said was quite sweet, and I love you for it. I have to tell you what's been bothering me." She pushed aside their plates. "Let's go sit on the couch."

Through her tears she told Cole about the offer. Cole held her in his arms as she sobbed.

"Beth, an opportunity like this doesn't present itself everyday. You have to take it, because if you don't, you would always wonder about it later. Besides, there's only 300 miles between us—that's just a five hour drive. After you learn your schedule we could figure out when we can be together. And Beth... I want that very much."

Beth brightened, smiling through her tears. "Me too."

34

Scott was in his office, conferring with a client when Kory came home.

Simone waved to her as she passed. She was carrying a bulky package, so she didn't stop but went upstairs to their bedroom. It was the new laptop computer she had bought for Scott. His birthday was two weeks away, and she had wanted to get him a gift he could really use. The store had done a beautiful job of wrapping it. She slid it under the bed and out of sight.

Earlier, a man had called the office and asked to speak with Scott. Simone said, "Mr. St. Germain is in a meeting with a client. Could he return your call?"

"That's strange," Simone told Scott later. "The man refused to give his name, but said he would call later and hung up. I checked the caller ID, but the display showed that the information was unavailable."

"Don't lose sleep over it, Simone," Scott assured her.

~

Manny had figured he should exchange his Illinois plates with local ones, so his car wouldn't be as noticeable. The trick was to find a car with current tags that wasn't being used regularly. One afternoon, he drove around looking for the right vehicle to use. Finally he located a salvage yard where several cars were parked in front, their *For Sale* signs displayed prominently. He scanned them: one was covered in dust, indicating it had been there for a time.

Later, after dark and when the business had closed, Manny went back. He parked a block away and walked to the car he'd noticed before and quickly removed the front and back plates. In a city park, he stopped under the trees, attached the Wisconsin plates to his car, and tossed the Illinois plates into the river.

He looked forward to finishing off the attorney and his girlfriend. He'd had enough of the hick town. He wanted to get back to Chicago where the real action was.

Beside her, Kory's cell phone was buzzing on the desk. The display showed it was her realtor. "Hello?" she said.

"Good news, Kory. We have a full price offer with no contingencies and a quick escrow. It's just what you asked for."

"Are you sure the buyer is qualified?"

"Yes."

"Then I accept."

"Great! I'll send you an electronic contract by email. There are instructions on where to sign and initial. I'll deposit the earnest money with the title company and get started on escrow."

"I'll look forward to receiving it. Thank you for your work," Kory said and they both clicked off. She hadn't imagined that it could be this easy.

Scott had finished the appointment with his client and sauntered out into the reception area. "Simone, has Kory called?"

"She's upstairs, boss." Simone didn't look up from her computer. Scott started toward the steps.

"Kory?" I called out. "Are you here?" As I entered the bedroom I could hear the shower running. I hurriedly undressed and slipped into the shower with her. She was startled at first, but settled into my arms, welcoming me with a warm kiss.

"Got time for a quickie?" She smiled through the soap and shampoo as she reached down between my legs.

"I'll make time." I picked her up to my waist and slid myself into her. I stepped forward until her back was braced against the shower wall. Her legs were wrapped around me, pushing me in deeper. She exploded first then it was my turn. "My, that was a quickie," I said and laughed. It was under five minutes.

"Speed demon," she laughed.

"I have a plan...."

"You mean, besides this?"

"Yes. Let's pack an overnight bag. We can have dinner at The Crew's Quarters and sleep overnight on the yacht."

"Let's bring a bottle of wine. I feel like being real naughty tonight." Kory grinned, her sly come-hither smile that had always turned me on.

"You're on, but right now I need to get back to work." I dressed, straightened myself up as best I could, and went back down stairs.

The moment Scott left, Kory's cell phone buzzed again. The display showed an unknown caller. "Hello?" she answered. No one spoke at first. "Who's calling please?"

"My name's Wilbur Sawgrass. I'm calling about the house you're selling on Raymond Road. Could you show it to me, if that'd be possible?"

"I'm sure we could make some arrangements, Mr. Sawgrass. However I have plans for this evening, perhaps tomorrow morning—say about eleven?"

"Fine. See ya' then."

There was an odd sting in the voice of this "Mr. Sawgrass." Kory went downstairs. "Is Scott busy?" she asked Simone.

"He's on the phone, but he shouldn't be long," Simone said.

Kory could see him through the large office window.

Minutes later he waved to her. "Come on in," he called.

"I have an appointment tomorrow to show Papa's house. I'd like you to come with me if you have the time. There's something in this man's voice that makes me feel like I wouldn't want to be alone with him," Kory said.

"Really?" Scott looked up at her, puzzled. If anyone felt strong and sure of herself, it was Kory Sims.

"Call me crazy." Kory shrugged. "But it's just a gut feeling."

"Okay, I'll go with you," Scott said.

Manny lay on his bed wondering what kind of plans they had this evening. "I'll check on them and see where they go," he muttered to himself.

Later, he parked down the street from Scott's home and waited. Thirty minutes later a Jeep backed out of the driveway; there were two people inside. It wasn't quite dark yet and traffic was light. Manny followed the Jeep to a restaurant called The Crew's Quarters. The parking lot was nearly full so he parked across the street, anticipating a wait of over an hour. He would have plenty of time to go back to the motel and gather up his money envelopes, his personal things, and most of all, his gun.

When he returned the Jeep was still there. *I'll wait as long as it takes, because tonight is the night they'll meet their end.*

35

When we'd finished dinner, I asked Kory, "Did you bring the wine?"

"Oh, yes. It's on ice in the cooler."

She'd reached under the table, caressing my leg, then higher and higher until I responded to her touch. I smiled at her. It was time to ask for the check.

As much as I enjoyed the attention, I asked her to stop. It would have been difficult to stand with a large object struggling to get out from my pants and not be noticed. By the time the waiter had returned I had myself under control.

We stopped at a couple of tables on the way out, greeting friends and old clients and, of course, introducing Kory.

As we walked across the parking lot Kory took my

arm. It was a beautiful evening: stars danced across the sky and tiny lights from lightning bugs flashed all around us. Now, the *Snow Flake* awaited us.

We parked close to the fence near the entrance to our dock. I opened the back hatch of the Jeep and picked up our overnight bags and the cooler. Hand in hand, we walked to the security gate. I swiped my card, and the gate clicked open. All seemed quiet as we passed the other boats. When we arrived at the *Snow Flake* I took particular notice of Bentley's yacht: it was completely dark, and no one was aboard.

"Honey, wait here while I turn on the cabin lights so you can see your way."

Kory followed me aboard and went directly to the master stateroom. She closed the curtains and put away what she had brought. I turned on some soft music and closed the curtains in the main cabin's salon. Kory came through to the main cabin dressed in a sheer, lacy peignoir that was very sexy. She looked stunning—she always did.

The drive to the marina was a short one, and Manny followed them slowly. He parked and watched from his car as the curtains on the yacht were pulled shut. It didn't appear that they were going anywhere. "This will be perfect," he muttered.

He dug around until he found the waterproof bag he had used before. Manny screwed the silencer on the muzzle of his gun, stuck it in the bag, and snapped shut the watertight seal. He removed his shoes, socks, and shirt and left them in the car. Far in the distance, he could hear the hum of the traffic crossing the interstate bridge.

After adjusting the bag and strap around his shoulders, Manny secured it across his chest, allowing him to keep his hands free for swimming. He crept along the grassy bank until he reached the end of the fence and open water. He eased down into the harbor and began swimming out to deeper water. He knew exactly where the *Snow Flake's* slip was located. At the end of the pier he grasped the metal ladder and pulled himself up and onto the firm planks of the pier. After waiting a few minutes and letting the water drip from his clothes and body, he advanced toward the yacht. First, he removed the bag, opened it, and pulled out the gun. The moonlight cast eerie shadows, reflecting off the water that was as smooth as glass. He stepped aboard cautiously, not wanting the boat to move.

Manny had been aboard many times when Mo was the owner and knew the yacht's layout. Soft music flowed from inside. He peeked through the port; the curtains were open just enough. St. Germain and his girl were walking aft toward the stateroom hand in hand, turning off the cabin lights behind them. Manny waited in the darkness; he wanted the moment to be right. He advanced slowly though the main cabin to the dimly lit stateroom with the biggest bed. He stopped to listen for only a moment. The sounds of their lovemaking blended with the music. Then he burst into the cabin, gun aimed at them, his finger pressed to his lips. "Shh!"

~

Kory was trying to cover herself with a sheet. She looked terrified. Awkward as it was, I tried to shield her and placed myself in front of her.

"Who the fuck are you? And what do you want?" I jumped up, grasping at another sheet.

The crazy man in my yacht's cabin said nothing. He motioned for Kory to come to him. I held her back.

"If you don't come here to Manny, I'll shoot lover boy right between the eyes." The intruder extended his arm so the gun was even closer to me.

"But… But—I don't have any clothes on," Kory said.

He chuckled. "Ya' think I've never seen a naked woman before?"

She slipped from behind me and walked slowly toward him. He spun her around to face me, keeping his arm around her neck. With his other hand he pressed the muzzle of the gun to her temple.

"Now, asshole, I want you to untie this boat and take us out into Green Bay. If you try anything, I will kill this pretty little thing. Do you understand?"

I nodded and left the cabin. Out on deck I cast off the ropes tied around the dockside cleats and came back into the main cabin. Manny was sitting down with Kory on his lap, the gun still to her head. With his other hand, he was fondling her breasts. Kory was crying; her eyes met mine, pleading for help.

Hoping that the son-of-a-bitch would make a mistake soon, I started the engines, turned on the running lights, and maneuvered the yacht out of the marina in the darkness, following the channel markers. We traveled slowly up the river toward Green Bay.

My cell phone was in my pants, which were on a chair in our stateroom. I couldn't use the yacht's radio without Manny noticing. But I'd keep him talking. "You must have something against me. Why else would you be doing this?"

"I don't have anything against you personally, but my boss does. You're just a paycheck to me," Manny said.

"Are you the one who's been doing all whose strange things to us?"

"Yeah, that's me, counselor." He laughed. It was a harsh, evil laugh.

"Please let me put some clothes on," Kory begged.

"What for, baby? You'll both be dead in an hour. Go sit over there, where I can see ya' both." Manny waved his gun in the air.

Kory crossed to a stool on the bridge and picked up my windbreaker that I'd left there when we boarded.

I would try to distract him. "Who's your boss?"

"I don't see how it can hurt, seeing you won't be able to tell anyone. Do you remember hearing the name Mo?"

"You mean the guy that used to own this yacht?"

"Yeah. That's the one. He told me you and that other guy named Claude cheated him in a card game. I killed that guy already." Manny looked proud of himself.

"I'll have to admit you certainly have been annoying," I said

"Actually, it's been kinda fun," Manny said.

"What's your name?" I asked.

"Manny. Manny Bruso," he said without any hesitation.

"You live around here?" I asked as I pulled back, bit by bit, slowing the *Snow Flake*'s speed gradually and hoping he wouldn't notice.

"Nah. I'm from the big city of Chicago," Manny said with pride.

"So... how are we going to die? Do you plan on dumping our bodies overboard and heading for Chicago on the *Snow Flake?*"

"Well, counselor, since you asked. I'm tying you up first, and I'm going to let you watch me rape your friend here."

Kory screamed and ran toward him. He brushed her aside, hitting her with the back of his hand.

I didn't have a chance to do anything to help her—he was too far away.

"No, my plan is simple. After I dispose of you two, I'm undoing the dinghy, the rubber raft. Then I'll shoot a bunch of holes in this tub so it'll sink." He laughed. "Then I'll head back to shore in the raft, pick up my car, and drive to Chicago for my big payday!"

I jerked the wheel hard to the left and pushed the throttle forward to full speed. It caught Manny off guard, sending him flying across the space and landing against a coffee table. His head came down hard against the edge. He lost his grip on the gun, and I tried to pounce on him.

While we were struggling, I shouted, "Kory! Get the gun!" He was on his back, and I was punching him with everything I had.

"I can't find it!" she called to me.

The *Snow Flake* was going in a tight circle; it was difficult to stand up, let alone walk.

"When you find it, go to the helm! See if you can straighten us out!" I yelled.

After I kicked him in the groin, he vomited and quit fighting immediately. My anger had not subsided yet.

He'd killed my friend, he'd destroyed my RV, and most of all, he'd terrorized the woman I loved. I kicked him a couple more times for good measure and then hit him in the face hard enough to break his nose.

Kory still had not found the gun but had managed to get to her feet and then straightened out our course. She'd cautiously pulled back the throttle, but we were at least progressing at a reasonable speed. I looked around and at last found the gun.

"I'll get some duct tape and rope from the supply cabinet," I shouted and handed the gun to Kory. "Don't shoot him though. We need him alive."

After he was completely secured, I located my cell phone and called Cole. "We've got him—Claude's murderer and the guy who was going to kill us." Then I explained what had happened.

"I can't believe it," he said. "We'll meet you at the marina."

36

Cole and several other officers met us at the dock. They had shown the good sense not to arrive with emergency lights on, which would have only caused confusion and attracted attention. The officers helped tying off the boat. "No one go aboard yet," Cole ordered.

Kory had gotten dressed. She was still trembling, and one of the officers helped her to the dock.

"Do we need an ambulance?" Cole asked.

"No. Just minor injuries," I answered. "And Manny has a broken nose, I believe."

Cole came aboard and started taking pictures of where the brawling took place and of Manny Bruso. When he was finished, I helped unwind the rope from Manny's legs and stood him up.

"This piece of shit has a lot to tell you," I said

"And I'll be happy to listen," was Cole's snappy rejoinder.

The other officers walked Manny to their awaiting patrol unit and placed him in the back.

"Put him in an interview room. I'll be back there in a few minutes," Cole told them.

"We'll come with you and give our statements," I said. "Did you find his car yet?"

"You bet. It was easy." Cole laughed. "It was the only one left in the parking lot besides yours."

It was a little after midnight when we arrived at the Marinette Police Station.

"We could really use a nice, hot cup of coffee," Kory said. She was shivering, partly from fear.

"I'll make a new pot. This one's at least six hours old," one of the officers said.

Cole led the way. "Let's go to an interview room."

"Do you mind if I record our conversation?"

"Not a problem." I looked to Kory and she nodded.

"Okay. Start from the beginning," Cole said

For the next twenty minutes, Kory and I told him about the events of the night.

"So he's responsible for Claude Curry's murder.... I'll be damned!" Cole shook his head in disbelief. "When this gets out the whole town will rest a lot easier."

"And the guy from Chicago that you played cards with that night is this guy's boss—a hired hit man."

"Have you found his wallet yet for an ID?" I asked.

"Yeah, he has three of them, two Illinois driver's licenses and one from Florida. One is 'Sam Smith' and the others are as Manny Bruso. I'm willing to bet Bruso is the real name," Cole said.

"What are you going to do about Michael O'Bannon?" I asked.

"I'll call Chicago PD. I'll tell them what we have and request that they arrest him."

"Digger told me he's a pretty slippery character. I hope he doesn't have friends in the right places and get wind of this ahead of time." I was worried. That kind of thing could happen and did happen, all too often.

"I'll make the call right now, before interviewing Mr. Bruso." Cole turned and left our interview room.

Mo did have friends in the Chicago PD.

Ten minutes after Cole made his call Mo's cell phone rang. Detective First Grade Frankie Lewis whispered the news into his phone.

"Thanks, Frankie. I'll take care of it right away, I appreciate your call. Of course, there'll be something extra for you." Then Mo dialed a number he'd memorized, his backup plan.

"Yeah... what ya' need, Mo?" a sleepy voice answered on the third ring.

"Snake, you need to be in Marinette, Wisconsin, as soon as you can. I need you to put a bullet in Manny Bruso's head. Make sure he's dead, then get the hell out of there. He's at the police station. There'll be ten grand for your trouble," Mo clicked off. His contact Snake left Chicago thirty minutes later.

Cole and another officer entered the interview room where Manny was waiting and the interview began.

"Today's date is July 29, 2010, in Marinette, Wisconsin, Police Department headquarters. I'm Cole Dominic and along with officer Stanley Potter, we will be interviewing a Mr. Manny Bruso." He paused. "Sir, I'm recording our conversation during this interview. Do you understand?"

Manny nodded.

"Sir, you need to respond out loud."

"Yes, I understand," Manny said.

"Is your true name Manny Bruso?"

"Yes."

"Do you currently reside at 57741 W. Howard Street, Chicago, Illinois?"

"Yes."

"Were you hired by a Michael O'Bannon to kill Claude Curry?"

Manny didn't answer at first. He knew if Mo learned that he'd been caught he was as good as dead.

"You have to promise to protect me," he pleaded. "If I talk, I'll never make it to the courtroom alive." The man was looking very nervous, perspiration beading on his forehead.

"We'll put you up in a safe house and have our armed officers stationed outside."

"Is that the best you can do?" Manny asked. The panic in his voice had ratcheted up a notch.

"Afraid so, Mr. Bruso."

"Don't you guys have some kind of witness program?"

"No. Manny, just the Feds have that program. You're not a witness, you're the bad guy."

"Oh, yeah. You're right." Manny spoke softly, begging. "But you still got to protect me."

"We will if you tell us what you know." Cole was getting impatient with Manny.

"Yeah, I killed that guy Claude Curry. I cut his throat in his garage. It was on Mo's orders. I also harassed that attorney and his chick."

"What's the attorney's name?" Cole asked.

"Uh… Mr. St. Germain, I think. I don't know the babe's name, but she's a looker." He was smiling, pleased with himself again.

The rest of the interview went smoothly. Kory and I had been standing outside the interviewing room, watching through the one way glass and listening to his confession. For the part we were involved in, it was pretty much on spot. We left the station and went home.

In the morning, Manny was allowed to shower; later, standard jail fare breakfast was brought to him. Cole had ordered an SUV to be brought around back but then stopped by Manny's cell. "Hey, Manny there's something else I want to ask you about."

"Oh, yeah? What?"

"Let's go back to the interview room and get it recorded like yesterday."

"Okay," Manny said.

Cole started the recorder and went through the same process as the day before. "Manny, when we searched your car we found a lot of cash. Strangely, we found eight marine emergency flares.... We also found some women's clothing. Two teddies to be exact. They're not exactly your style—or your size."

"Oh, yeah. I'm already going to get the maximum sentence. When you run the DNA you'll find out anyway. They belonged to the twin sisters I killed and buried out in a field." He shrugged, acting matter of fact about what he'd done. "They were whores anyway. No big loss."

Cole pushed up from his chair, then restrained himself. How he longed to beat this guy to a pulp. "Get him out of here," he muttered to one of his officers.

Manny was already wearing cuffs. Before they settled him into the van, the officers had also put ankle chains on him. The SUV pulled away with Manny sitting comfortably and secured appropriately in the back.

~

That morning Mo's man called Snake arrived in Marinette. His first order of business was to steal a car; then he had driven to the police station and parked across the street. When the SUV pulled out, Snake started following them and laughed. Those officers had no experience doing this kind of work. It would be easy, almost too easy.

Before arriving at the safe house, the driver pulled into a convenience store and went inside for three Slushies: one for each of the officers and one for Manny. Snake pulled in beside the SUV. He'd earlier put the silencer on his gun. He stepped out quickly, shooting the cop in the passenger seat and then firing two rounds into Manny's forehead, killing him instantly. He jumped back in the stolen car and sped off to where he had parked his own car. He wiped down the stolen car and left the area, being careful not to break any traffic laws.

Cole heard the frantic call come in from the officer who had been driving the SUV. "Officer down! Officer down!" he repeated. "Officer Bains is shot. I'm trying to give him first aid! Send an ambulance—Code three!"

"Shit!" Cole immediately called for roadblocks set up in all directions. Several officers were dispatched to the scene. No one at the convenience store had seen anything. The ambulance arrived and transported Officer Bains to the ER. Good news arrived later that he would survive.

"That just about blows our whole case," Cole said. "It's just hearsay now."

What Cole couldn't have known was that not all cops in Chicago were as corrupt as Frankie Daniels. Another detective already had had a wiretap on Mo's phones. The tap picked up the early morning call to Snake, a direct recoding of Mo ordering the hit on Manny. Mo was in deep shit and wouldn't be seeing the light of day for the rest of his life.

37

It was a pleasant Sunday afternoon, past the heat and humidity of summer. I was relaxing in my easy chair and reading one of Kory's novels when the doorbell rang. I was hesitant to answer, but then it rang again.

Kory was out back tending to her roses. She had planted some lovely new rose bushes in the garden, adding beauty to our house in so many ways.

I went to the door and opened it. To my surprise, it was Mr. and Mrs. Dunlap. I smiled and greeted them warmly. "Hello. Mr. Dunlap… Mrs. Dunlap. Please come in."

Bernard Dunlap shook my hand. "Thank you, but no. We were in town to put flowers on our Kelly's grave."

Sally Dunlap faced me, tears forming in her eyes. She sniffed once. "You know, she would have been eleven years old today."

"We just wanted to stop by and say thank you again for your help. And all your hard work on our behalf," Bernard said solemnly and Sally nodded.

"There's no need to thank me. We just had to convict the man for his crimes."

"We'll be on our way." They turned, waved good-bye, and left.

Too much had happened in the past months. Being personally threatened and fearing for my own life had almost driven the picture of the Hastings execution from my mind. Almost... but it would never fade. He had killed an innocent child, and justice was done.

Then I thought of the twins. Maybe their way of life wasn't the best, but they didn't deserve to die that way either. And their killer was gone from society now too.

I was still pondering justice, what was right, what was wrong, and the tragedies that surrounded us—that surrounded everyone—when Kory came in, finished with fertilizing the roses.

"You know," she said. "When I finished out there I brushed the dirt from my clothes and realized that K9 had been sitting there the whole time, just staring up at me."

I laughed. It was good to think about something else other than murder—like dogs and rose bushes.

"Well, I thought he looked lonesome," Kory said. "When I told him he probably needed a friend, he yapped a couple of times and spun around in a circle—like he understood me."

"You're probably right," I told her and then kissed her. "You're right about so many things. Let's go to the pet store."

The three of us climbed into the Jeep, and I got to thinking what that Jeep had witnessed over the past months and was glad that cars couldn't remember.

At the pet store, Kory was enchanted by a beautiful, white Bichon Frisé. We allowed K9 to get down in a playpen with her to watch how they might get along. It seemed like love at first sight.

We named her Chloe and took her home with us that day. Later that night as we lay in bed watching TV, the dogs hopped up onto our bed and sprawled about at our feet. K9 snuggled up to Chloe's soft white fur and closed his eyes.

We looked at each other. I put my arm around Kory, understanding how K9 felt. "Now our little family is complete."

The End

Acknowledgements

Every writer works alone to some extent, but each of us depends on the support of many others, sometimes too numerous to mention. Most importantly, I wish to thank my wonderful wife Marilyn, for her unwavering love, support, and patience. The motivation and inspiration provided by a group of like-minded writers has been invaluable, especially the encouragement of author Don Stevens. Many thanks to Lynn Cox for her friendship and help. Also, I'm especially grateful to Michaele Lockhart, my editor, fellow author, and friend, for her work and belief in me.

R. T. Wiley

About the Author

Former police officer and author R. T. Wiley brings over a decade's experience in law enforcement to his writing. From an urban police department in California to a county sheriff's department in Oregon, Wiley has lived the world that he writes about. Following his debut novel, *Seriously Flawed,* Wiley draws on his boating adventures on the Great Lakes for *Snow Flake.* Now retired, he resides in Chandler, Arizona, with his wife Marilyn.

Made in the USA
San Bernardino, CA
11 October 2016